The MK

The MK Myth

a walkable novel

Phil Smith & K

Published by:
Triarchy Press
Axminster, England

info@triarchypress.net
www.triarchypress.net

A catalogue record is available from the British Library.

Printed in the UK by TJ International Ltd., Padstow, Cornwall

Print ISBN: 978-1-911193-49-4

ePub ISBN: 978-1-911193-50-0

Tracing the Pathway and Phil Smith would like to record their thanks to all those who tested parts of *The MK Myth* route and shared their reflections: Andy Stansfield, Annabelle Shelton, Beatrice Jarvis, Bob Jarvis, Francesca Skelton, Hillie Edwards, Jane Stansfield, Jo Trotter, John Skelton, Kevin McConway, Lallie Davis, Mari Sved, Priya Chohan, Roisin Callaghan, Thomas Cuthbertson, Thomas Eke, Aaron James.

This work has been commissioned by Tracing the Pathway as part of their project Groundwork, a cross-arts platform and research project for and about Milton Keynes. *The MK Myth* also forms part of Pedalling Culture, a Cultural Destinations Fund programme funded by Arts Council England.

Supported using public funding by
ARTS COUNCIL ENGLAND

Milton Keynes Arts Centre

Contents

Introductory Note of Advice

We hope you enjoy reading and using this book. It is one of a number of manifestations since 2015 of Tracing the Pathway's Groundwork project in Milton Keynes. The idea of a 'novel for the city' arose after many days of walking in Milton Keynes and it reflects those origins.

The MK Myth can be read as a novel, walked or cycled as a route, read as you walk, read before walking, or read after walking. As a route, you can walk it or cycle it in stages and there are suggested starts and stops signalled in the text. These are only suggestions. If you are cycling, be prepared to carry or lift your bike, or leave it locked briefly, to access parts of the walk. If you are a very fit long-distance walker, you might just about walk the route all in one go, but it would be - literally - a marathon, and you would probably miss many of the things that slower, shorter walks will reveal.

The directions in the book are intended to be sufficient to get you around the route, but take an A-Z map with you if you feel happier that way, or use a GPS facility on your phone.

Some parts of the route go through very quiet, un-public places, and – although the likelihood of a threatening situation is very, very remote – not everyone feels confident in these spaces, so you might want to consider the option of walking with a companion or in a group.

Much of the route of *The MK Myth* is on accessible pavements and Redways, but not all of it. Short sections of the route are steep and uneven and there are some steps. At different times of year some of the ground will be wet and may be slippery. Take care, and if you are concerned about an incline or slipperiness, there are often alternatives that will keep you on the flat and allow you to pick up the route again a little further on. Remember that Milton Keynes is changing all the time; be alive to the possibility that some of the details of the directions might become out of date (a sign taken down or replaced, a gap mended) by new developments and you may need to keep your wits about you.

Wrap up warm or put on sun block as appropriate, and carry waterproofs if the weather forecast suggests you should. The route passes the occasional café, but you may want to take water and something to eat. Comfortable walking boots are recommended.

The MK Myth

The Sun rose in the east. The light ran along the lines of the traffic system and collected in hundreds of movies of the sky on the glass panes in Station Square. Fusing for a moment in the air above the Square a pulse of energy raced above the central boulevard. At that exact moment, by an uncanny synchronicity of security guards and management, early morning shop workers and market stall owners, the doors in Centre:MK were opened in a sequence that allowed a blast of wind, driven by the solar concentration, to rattle the tubular parts of the Circle of Light hung above the Midsummer Arcade. The bright dangle of cylinders shook slightly and each began to turn around its own axis creating a shimmering dragon of coppery light.

A group of early morning workers was gathering outside the Midsummer Place entrance to INTU, annoyed and confused. The large orange disk of concrete, on which they usually perched each morning for a final cigarette before the working day began, had been buried under a flowerbed contained within a grey wooden fence. One of the smokers, leaning over to toss her extinguished butt into the gap between the giant planter and the grey fence, caught a glimpse of orange just as the energy sweeping up the boulevard caught them all unawares. Those cigarettes still lit flared in showers of sparks like unhinged Catherine Wheels.

Confused by the absence of the Midsummer Oaks and the abjection of the magic structure of The Point, the energy burst from INTU, dodged the first buses, raced under Marlborough Gate, over Marlborough Street, down the 'leisure path' – ignoring ornamental fripperies – and burst along the ridge until, hitting the Light Pyramid in a white hot flash, it shot back into the sky. Other than a handful of rattled smokers, MK's alchemical moment had been missed by everyone else for another day. With one other exception...

For a single photon had detached itself at Station Square, deflected as it caught the cornea of the eye of a rat dodging between the shrubs below Elder Gate. In a flash – passing at a speed slightly less than c – it had reached the suburbs, bounced around Cranbourne Avenue as if it were in the Large Hadron Collider and flew off, dizzily losing all sense of direction, before penetrating a small gap between a pair of retro red and blue print Zephyr curtains in a large flat in one of the more fashionable of the city's developments and flashed through the pupil exposed by the flickering eyelid of a young female executive, K.

Her light sleep disturbed, K opened her eyes and groaned. She had beaten the alarm again. There was some satisfaction in the groan.

Throwing back the drapes, the bedroom filled with light, each particle of which was a lost opportunity. K stretched; she felt the balances of stiffness and looseness in her muscles.

K could never be quite sure about meaning. If she knew where it came from, and occasionally she did, she never knew where it went. The significance of the day was still up for grabs. That morning, when she woke, she was already alone. She straightened the bed clothes, threw a wine bottle into the waste bin and cleared away the dinner party things in her kitchen, sweeping crumbs from the work surface, and filled the coffee maker. She smiled to herself; a smile for no one else, about no one else.

She lit the flame, then turned it low.

Exciting times, she told herself. Today she would be pitching a detailed psychographic strategy to a number of potential clients around the city, a means to crafting clusters of preferences as a guide for campaigns of every kind; and something more.

K laughed.

Possibly at the realisation that she had no idea what most of these companies produced; probably nothing at all. There was always some theatre involved; all that recruitment, e-commerce videos, retail strategising, fencing and security, surveillance and data processing depended on everyone believing that everyone else was making something. Trust. She had a face that people trusted. A famous movie mogul once famously said that you could have everything if you could fake sincerity... in K's case that was unnecessary. She was the Joan of Arc of her pitch.

K laughed again.

Possibly at whether she had really said "let's get drunk and you can tell me your secrets".

She caught the coffee just as it threatened to spit all over the cooker.

As she frothed the milk, she checked the diary on her phone. Five meetings. She transferred the data to a satnav app and the meetings came up as the five points of a wonky star pinned to the city; industrial estates and offices in and around the centre. Minutes were ticking away, but she always made time for the first coffee.

Her first sip was for temperature. Perfect, like the rest of her life. Like everything she controlled. Since she had stopped making excuses for young white men the territory under her control had increased considerably. She had begun to enjoy the company of those who behaved as though her presence was a privilege not a recreation. She had begun to scare her bosses – in a good way – and they seemed to regard that as a transferable value.

The second sip – more of a gulp really – was all about the caffeine rush, the drive and thrust through the veins. The taste turning on the afterburners. The low flame had allowed the coffee grains to deeply infuse the water and now their psychoactive chemicals pervaded her central nervous system. She soaked in the feeling; holding her breath. The momentary oxygen deprivation, the sudden accumulation of carbon dioxide triggered extra pleasure centres, charging beta-endorphins around her brain.

Before the third sip she knew something was, not quite wrong, but altered.

In a mild panic, she began to routinise. She checked her things; then checked them again. She tried to remember the five meeting places and their order. She could not. They were in her phone; the machines would get her there, her five-pointed star was bright. As she dressed in the Paul Smith rip-off she had found online, she rehearsed her pitch, but, infuriatingly, the different parts refused to sit still in her memory, each one thrusting itself to the fore; then collectively racing back to their caves, feigning shyness. She could remember none of them. K stumbled as a heel caught in a trouser leg. Someone had put a fork in her head and stirred. She felt frightened. She padded round the flat followed by a phantom leopard – a spirit animal she had adopted from a self-help book. She settled herself, blanked her brain and rebooted.

Yet nothing reordered itself properly. It would eventually, she reassured herself of that. She calmed down by reminding herself of social faux pas, missed appointments and forgotten dates she had always manoeuvred her way around. While her mind was a blue screen of death, the best thing was to drive, subject herself to the top layer of the street hierarchy, tracing the V streets and the H ways that divided the uncrossed districts. Like the newly arrived blanks in her mind, she knew those local areas were full of something, but she had no idea of their order or arrangement or who lived there and what they cared about; she knew them by their data. Driving would reassert the original plan; return the whole to normal, re-establish the overall concept.

She blipped the car open with her key – some things were automatic – and belted up, then pressed down on the clutch and turned the ignition. She laid her head back on the rest in relief as the car immediately grumbled to life. She was connected. She turned out of her driveway and drove, as she always did, past the new houses, the local centre and out towards the grid, inserting herself at the first of eleven roundabouts that would bring her to the central zone and a preliminary meeting with her fellow exec-layer reps.

She was going to be very, very slightly late.

K's company – or rather the company that K worked for (she hoped to correct that shortly) – had unremarkable but serviceable offices beyond the V11; however, to mark the exceptional nature of the new service they would be selling from today, the company had chosen to move the early morning briefing to a meeting room at Jury's Inn.

The predictability of the city – a place without mistakes – was such that K experienced the roads as times to destinations rather than physical distances. The eleven verticals and ten horizontals did not exist in themselves; they were periods of waste between points of arrival and departure. K had never remarked any change of atmosphere between, say, V4 Watling Street and H6 Childs Way; instead she locked into the grid and the grid locked into her, ordering her day with its logical succession and dispersal of meetings, consultations, briefings, pitches and reports. The grid was her facilitator; along with a laser pointer and a laptop, the grid fitted her handbag, permeated a cocktail in the evening and structured her dreams in the darkness around worlds of various shades.

She briefly acknowledged, in passing, the anomaly of the A5 before reaching the Midsummer Roundabout; all that stuff about alignments. A city driven by the Sun. No. She was driving this city. K cut rightwards across the lanes of the boulevard, using the gash left by Upper Fifth Street and turned right past the parking spaces servicing The Hub, drifting gently down to the oval space, with the round pupil, outside Jury's Inn. The eye was empty, staring up at the cold blue sky.

K stopped her car outside the hotel's front entrance and ran in. She would leave a message at reception, ask them to phone up to the conference room and let her colleagues know that, once parked, she was on her way. But there was already a message waiting for her; they had left without her.

K shrugged aggressively at the receptionist. Things accelerated around; her mind raced.

As she jogged back to her motor, all cool exterior, imagining how climbing into a Tesla Model S might feel, she reached for her keys. Not in her bag, not in her hand, not in her jacket. She ran back inside the hotel. Not at reception. Ran back out. Not on the pavement. Not in the gutter. Not lying along any one of the spars issuing from the blank pupil, not in the eyelid, not in the eyebrow, nowhere. She had a spare set. Back at the flat. Get a taxi back to the flat. How would she get in without keys? Taxi to the next meeting? She reached to check the time on her phone. It was locked in the car. She could see it on the passenger seat. Should she smash the window? The list with the times and places of the five meetings was on the phone. She stepped backwards to take a swing at the window, but it might have been Fate or the Sun that took away her foothold and pushed her in the face, sending her tripping backwards, almost to the door of the hotel.

She turned to wave apologetically to the reception staff, but she was distracted by daffodils. All her lithe exterior had fallen away; she was open now.

The city lit up. It was like a map of yellow light, of dazzlingly bright routes; the five-tipped starmap of her meetings shone the brightest, its points nestling in spaghetti-like tangles of nervous wiring, pulsing with big data, set in a motherboard made of golden treacle. Maybe it was the coffee, a flashback to the morning's accidental oxygen deprivation, maybe it was the daffodils; the map was inside and outside K, it was imaginary and it was the city. Somehow K had spontaneously birthed a psycho-geographical chart, a projection of the city moving in all directions, emotionally and precisely. In a flash, K knew exactly how to get everywhere, and how those routes felt; not how she might feel about them, but how those routes were feeling right now before she traversed them. It was like being introduced to a transparent hydrozoa at a cocktail party: "let's get drunk, I can see right through you". The city was flirting with her. It was weird and she felt unwell and hyper-excited at the same time.

And scared. They were going to fire her for this. She always met and exceeded her targets, but complaints from other staff had started recently. For a company with the motto "innovate the next" they had a perverse fixation on the acceptable. Her options were narrowing.

She could walk...

She decided to follow the eastwards pointing spar of light from the sclera of the eye on the forecourt of Jury's

Inn; it lay exactly over the first point of her star. That was fortuitous. There. It was as simple as that; she had a plan, the whole city was seared into her hippocampus. Things were starting to make sense again. She was over the worst of the morning's wobble. This had been happening more often recently, these blank patches. She had tried to fill them with other people, with dating, with social excursions with her colleagues. They filled her time, she always enjoyed herself, but the blank patches were untouched; they were mysteries to which other people were not the solution. Nor were they her fault. She had faith in herself; she felt the shadow of the phantom leopard of the prosperity gospel, she embraced its positive thoughts, and she would set out to get to her meetings on time, make her pitches, seal her deals and drive this city from its paths. One step would lead to another. There was no sense in making things any more complicated than they needed to be.

A blue Perspex and grey synthetic stone chequerboard, set in the pavement to the side of Jury's Inn, meant something. K had no idea what, but the position of a cigarette butt in the margins of one of the blue squares might be significant. She duly noted and filed it. She knew, of course, that such details had no *real* meaning. There were so many of them, how would you assemble all the implications? But just noticing a little thing like that could be part of a greater strategy for her to follow. The devil, this time, would *not* be in the detail, she thought, but in the whole effing devil.

K turned down Cresswell Lane; because to make a real journey you do not walk in a straight line, you make decisions, you choose left and right, left then right, left and left and left again, but eventually you choose a right before you complete the circle. The lane was like a ravine; a man hidden in a doorway manifested as a hand and a phone.

There was a terrible smell, as if a rat had died in the yellow skip full of table tops, or maybe in the dark green bush that looked immune to seasons; she savoured its unnatural nature for a moment, but the smell was too much. Even as she moved away, she felt the odour catch a lift on her clothes. Her leopard spirit would hunt the ghost rat, gobble it down. She was only a few metres into her first journey, yet she had come so far from the shiny facades of Jury's, Browns and the Hub. The sickening aura dissipated, but the ghost of the ghost would haunt her. Rats in a modern city were not real things; that problem had been sorted out in the nineteenth century, surely; but the idea of them was harder to get rid of.

K changed her mind.

There was a giant rats' nest, right there!

In her years of driving around the grid, working for a number of companies, K had often noticed different episodes of a yellowing space between the giant banks of reflective glass. This, however, was a monster, an earth mound as long and as wide as a soccer pitch. It was sparsely covered with brush and a sickly kind of grass. It might once have been a prehistoric burial barrow or a massive pile of builder's spoil from the foundations of the Argos offices. Beside it was a road to nowhere, blocked at both ends by weighted plastic barriers, an expanse of concrete wall, forbidding wire fences, featureless pillars and an enigmatic tunnel to somewhere oblique; the walls of glass on the far side of the wasted space gave it the feel of a dystopian sci-fi set, a part of a controlled experiment conducted under fictional laboratory conditions. K wondered what...

TEMPORARY ELEVATION

...hidden in the fabric of the car park, meant – was it a message about what was happening to her? She felt inexplicably elated, as if she was in conversation with architecture and soil heaps.

Walk 1

Suggested start point: Jury's Inn Hotel, Midsummer Boulevard

Estimated walking time: 2 hours

Start at Jury's Inn Hotel on Midsummer
Boulevard, with your back to the central
railway station. For a few metres walk up
Midsummer Boulevard and then turn right,
after Browns, down Cresswell Lane.

One of the thorny brambles reached through the wire mesh
of the fence and snagged on the arm of K's jacket, swinging
her around before letting her go. The waste was talking
back, trying to hold her attention; walking was not just a
velocity, it was a reciprocal vulnerability.

Four plastic bollards of different sizes and colours stood
across the top of a little rising side road to her left. K burst
through their cordon, and up, between two stubby needle
palm trees, onto a bare concrete platform. Despite the
fringes of rough grass and a shallow pool of rainwater, K
had a sense of its importance as a spiritual place. A sparse
altar; an empty table awaiting the coming feast, the base,
the plane. From the platform, she gazed out over all the
abjection and obstruction around her, and she felt strong.
As if she had already 'got somewhere'. The platform
afforded her a good view of the giant metal struts holding
up the Bannatyne building. K was not usually given to
wondering about her immortal soul, or anyone else's, but
she had never ever considered that a city, or a pile of soil,
might have one. That there might be a spiritual quality in
all of the things that other people rubbished. That in the
backstage of the city's centre there were secrets about the
Whole Thing. K's business was all about dematerialisation,
breaking people down into binary code; but what if a spirit-
infused matter persisted in holding everything up?

> At the end of Cresswell Lane turn left up the
> pavement parallel to Avebury Boulevard with
> the wasteland immediately on your left
> behind the fence. Just beyond the turning
> into the service road on the left there is a rise
> onto a concrete platform; if accessible, stand
> on it for a short while.

Everything is cars, for example, she thought. Life is all a kind of parking. K wasn't sure what she meant. A kind of putting off, putting away, putting to one side. She thought of the friends from her work at last night's dinner party, the email she should write to her mother, the lovely photographer she was dating; so considerate of her needs that he made her suspicious. These were the things she parked when she was working. At those times, parts of her life stood still, in a parking bay. Like she was now. She had parked herself.

> Walk back down from the concrete platform,
> cross Avebury Boulevard and down South
> Sixth St., turning left across the car park.

The green portal with a luxuriance of foliage got her moving again. A great floppy beast of ivy, hanging off the trunks and boughs of trees and lolloping over some kind of utility building, smothering its bricks and painted door; at odds with the right-angles and restrictive boxes of the car park. How could such anomalies exist within a rational plan, unless the fabric of the plan consisted of and contained such anomalies? She had to stop herself doing that, K thought to herself. Breaking out with a new thought and then turning it into a prison.

An overcoat had been hung on one of the brick pillars of the office building next to the rampant foliage, as casually as if it were in the front hall of a colleague's flat or thrown over the back of an armchair. Under the overhang of the covered passage was a large sheet of cardboard, snug to the glass window of an office, and a sleeping bag. Sellotaped to the office window was a printed notice. K assumed it would be an ultimatum, but it addressed the homeless person and informed them politely that they should leave any valuable belongings stacked neatly under the notice, from where they would be removed and stored safely in the offices, redeemable on request, during a period of general exterior cleaning. Despite its civility, K sensed a threat in its calm charity, that maybe the generosity smoothed the way for a disinfecting of the space in more ways than one? She was often expected to write similar mundane prose that hid a sting. But there was no real evidence of that, and K hurried on, wondering why she was being sucked into the concerns of this homeless person, worried that from now on she would be haunted not only by the smell of a dead rat, but by the anxieties of an imagined rough sleeper. She did not want to walk as one of a crowd. Empathy was the last thing she needed right now.

Go through the gap between the red MacIntyre building on the left and a lighter yellowish-brown building on the right.

A massive shock of pink blossom. It was spring at last, and K was only now noticing; she was a latecomer to a latecoming season. Where was her spring?

Turning down South Seventh Street, K unexpectedly caught sight of Xscape out of the corner of her eye; how did it come to be there? She had slithered down its snow slope; she had been to its bars – Revolution (stupid name) and The Moon Under Water; she had been taken to various superhero movies and she had sat in seats that shook at the collapse of CGI'd buildings. Fearful of giving the eyeball any rest, those movies despised anything solid. But until now she had never considered the grossly inflated silverfish as being an entity in itself. Looked at in that way, even from so far off, the building loomed malevolently and inscrutably. It seemed sinister for being a spectacle that expressed nothing. Yet it also had a 'life' that was separate from the sum of all of its services and its entertainments. It had a life-in-itself that diminished K's.

When people looked at her in the street, from a similar distance, they did not see a life-in-itself like that in her. That would only come with celebrity. Oh, she had plans, even notoriety was investable, but until then her profession would be discreet and self-contained and even self-effacing; for all her sharp corners, she never betrayed a confidence. She had integrity. That was not what she thought about herself; that was what her competitors said about her.

Glancing nervously towards the cyclopean metal-slug, trying to avoid it noticing her, she was afraid of what the fallen silver cone might do once it began to satisfy its self-life.

> Once through the buildings, turn right down
> South Seventh St., then right down the path
> beside the next (also yellowish-brown) building.

She pulled up. Not just the bad feeling from the huge silver bug-building. The trees were in on it too, this life-sucking thing. She sensed they were trying to pull her in. No less than Xscape they had their own agendas; she was being lured off the map by the magnetic personality of landmarks and by paths that did not consider themselves as simple connecting spaces between parking lots and receptions. She was stuck again; after the initial rush of her journey she was stuttering. She would be late.

Frantically scrabbling about in the shrubs was a young Asian businessman. K wanted to speak with him. Had he dropped his keys too? Was he hunting a rat? Or maybe he had also lost his phone? Or lost his way? Maybe they could help each other? But she had to get on; they were waiting for her at the offices in Fox Milne.

For a long time now, she had wanted to belong to a majority, to instinctively conform, she had thought of her sales and her winning contracts as entry tickets to something that already existed; that her forward momentum would eventually loop back to something good that was always there. But recently she had begun to suspect that there was nothing to loop back to and that everyone had to make up everything as they went along. She could join clubs, of course, social circles, cultural associations; she imagined that the young man in the suit and tie could plug her into a host of new circuits, but, as always, she felt the fear of losing the opportunities already waiting for her and hurried on.

Once she got to Fox Milne she would tell them; together they were going to transform the substance of the city from the smoothly operating mechanism of the grid to a softly sensitive database-organism driven through a fluid of social potential by a full body of tentaculate algorithms. They would transcend existing social units in favour of free-forming clusters of opinions and predilections. This spelled an end to predatory friendships and relationships of subservience and the beginning of preference clusters as the building blocks of a new urban humanity sustained on tracks of data plugged into a new transportation grid for the city. She would remove the human element. She knew she was running loose from her presentation, but the words kept coming... Instead of the people going to the commodities and services, the services and commodities would be coming to them, by dissolving materials into data and by transporting what could not be dissolved on driverless delivery systems.

Clustering was the spiritual reward they could all reap if they were willing to make the leap to the next generation of informational exchange through structures of virtual and augmented realities, a wholly individuated, socially democratic technology; not a third way, but a way to the power of three! What manifested now as identity-anxiety would become a fiscal currency; impostor syndrome was tomorrow's cosplay, online was about to become mainline. Information would run – quite literally – through the veins and settle in the nerves, just as pioneers had once settled in Australia or the Wild West; purchases would be triggered direct from feelings, satisfactions direct from desires. She was signalling the end of the visual 'market stall' economy: no more of that extravagant nonsense on the face of Xscape, no more tiny screens fixating people's lives – replacement bio-mechanical eyes would be installed. Very soon there would be no secrets. Handheld devices would only be exchanged among small retro clusters of eccentrics. Thingness and sensibility would come back into fashion; old food vans and robot drones would visit the estates to deliver umbycords and pods, drilling bioports on request, distributing sensations and loyalties as ice creams were once vended. 'Social media' would simply and abruptly disappear, because under her plan all media would be social!

K pulled up short, scared like a horse at a tall fence, or one of those crazy people who walk the same stretch of pavement over and over. It was not just the new ideas ripping up the old her; it was the trees and what they were up to. She needed to get down the pathway, step over the panicking young businessman still hunting for his phone. She felt her own levels of adrenalin rising; they were not helping her. The path was shaped like the aisle of a church and some force wanted to walk her up it. No way! She needed to get to the estate at Fox Milne – get onto Grafton Street, then Chaffron Way and turn left along Tongwell Street, still thinking like a driver – but she could see clearly that this path would have an altar at the end of it; and she refused to be the sacrifice again!

The white globes of the street lamps floated free from their blue posts. The first tree on the right had two huge eyes and branches that reached out in amazed desire. She ran.

Racing out of alignment, the grid began to recalibrate to her. Her orientation was skewed to the lattice of paths and roads, H's and V's. Bang! It slammed down, in the middle of the path, a blue post with a floating white globe, brazenly confronting her; tree-aisle-maw and woody bridegroom behind her. She dodged around the cylindrical brain on the lamp post – she had no idea what kind of a shape she was in, but it was more interesting than a cylinder – and swept through the porte-cochère!

They would not let her off that easily again. To the left was Xscape, its giant face like that of a monster woodlouse, an ancient primitive thing that just by age had grown to power, that had no manners, no niceness, no real heart, a creeping under-thing with lots of legs, an Accumulation Monster with an eyeless face, vents in place of pupils. Its indifference would carry on haunting her, converting her natural goodness into sameness... Oh!

A Wall-E drone thing trundled across the pavement in front of her, chaperoned by two burly minders. They paid K no attention, but made notes about her. This diverted her attention away from the Bug-Palace and to a parking space accommodating a hearse. It was an odd idea; that people might die in offices. Places mostly emptied of human actions: there was no birth, sleep, dinner parties, theatre, sport, very little sex in offices. They were sending her a signal: "take on the grid and we can drive you away, any time... we'll send a drone without chaperones next time..."

> **When you reach the path with the trees on both sides in front of you, turn left down the path towards Childs Way, go through the porte-cochère and take the underpass beneath Childs Way.**

The people of the city approaching were deceptively normal; two guys, one black and one Asian, wearing lanyards over their bright shirts and subtler jumpers, their restrained jackets jarring with the rest of them. The black guy was checking his phone, while the Asian guy was swinging a lunch bag and staring ahead, as if he had something to look forward to. Both looked as if they were preparing to laugh. A younger woman was in their trails; nothing to do with them, part of the general conspiracy of the grid. She had long black hair and was dressed entirely in black, except for cheap but elegant beige shoes. An elderly white man, with white hair, black leather jacket and blue jeans was walking with his back to K, he was swinging a blue plastic shopping bag distended by what K imagined to be the necks of bottles and the rounded plastic corners of processed food packaging, as if struggling entities were pushing against the membrane. This was the first human monster she had encountered today, but she knew there were still plenty of these anachronistic behemoths around, smuggling home hideous embryos, desperate to break into the life cycle before the technology closed off their last way in. She had to get to Fox Milne quickly to warn them; any corporation with a profitable demographic client-base demurring at the first laws protecting the human rights of emoji would experience the same devastating effects on market share as non-specialising homophobic and transphobic corporations.

K found the darkness of the underpass comforting. It was from that darkness that each of these people had come. A beautiful thing they all shared: monsters, embryos, execs and office staff. This was a healing space that the drivers never experienced! A repeated bathing in shadows – she had not realised this before – was why the faces of the two young men shone as they stepped into the light. It was not the Devil Sun, but an inner shining of darkness, as a piece of polished coal could shine; it was a kind of fire that these people had, the black hair of the girl the same, glistening, as she took something from the shadows with her into the sunlight.

The plaque above the underpass was missing. There was a mark where it had shaded the concrete from the Sun. K did not know where she was going. She could not read the meaning of it and when she entered the underpass she felt the darkness sweep into her, as the world at the other end of the tunnel exploded in brightness. She shimmied as she stepped into the light again, as if she had been trained to avoid the Sun by the lightness of her footwork, and scampered up the verge on her left, skidding a little on the flowerless dandelions, scared that something – maybe an insect leg of Xscape or a ray of the Sun or one of those trees that marched in pairs – might catch her by the ankle and pull her back.

She could not bring herself to stop a passer-by or call at a house and ask for directions; she dare not even walk between the houses in case she found herself, impossibly and suddenly, home again, with no key to get in... where did she live in relation to where she was now? How many people, absent from their flats or houses, could at any moment point in the exact direction that would get them home? 5%? If that? No one knows where they are. For herself, without the view through the windscreen, K would never recognise the roads home! How would she ever get back? And why was she thinking about home when she needed to be thinking about work! She had pitches to make. It was all fine. She was going cross-country, taking the sneaky short cuts only the rats knew. She laughed for a fourth time. She was part of an entirely other species now.

Pushing through the low spiky shrubs, the shock of the cars, so loud and close, struck her in a wave. This was what being close to the outsides of cars was like, big and metal. Inside they were such quiet and self-contained things, with no relationship to anything, like bedsits on wheels. With their sound systems and satnavs, the only things they related to were satellites. But they were aggressive, they could kill you if you stepped into their path; K remembered being a child. Her mother had never walked. K had been brought up on the inside of cars. Her father sometimes washed and polished the outside of his, but he did that alone or took it to a garage to be done. It was his 'me time', he said. He liked the freedom and loneliness the car gave him. K had had no idea that cars had relationships with people. She reeled back into the trees, while the Xscape Bug directed the cars down Childs Way. The moment had put her back in her body.

Pushing through another layer of low grasping shrubs and ineffectual small trees, K picked her way down to a large expanse of green. Stepping onto it felt like standing on the rug of the world, but someone was pulling it away; the rock and the hard soil and the pillars of molten whatever that glued the globe together had gone mushy. The grass was packed with squidgy mosses, sinking in a few inches when you stepped on them, tiny daises spread thinly about the green like dots in a story that meant "not sure…", "not completed…"

The language inside K's head was getting more ecological, more organic, more like the work of a comic book colourist – not necessarily a good thing as it might start evolving in ways that were not in K's own interests.

Once through the underpass immediately cut left up the grass, onto the verge alongside Childs Way and then bear right through the trees onto a large patch of grass, heading for its far right corner (at the corner of Sutcliffe Avenue and Boycott Avenue).

K's relief at stepping off the grass onto the metalled path was undermined by the large black puddles forming across it, fed from concrete drains that were set into the grass to her left, as if a clogging had overloaded the system. The tops of two of the drains were missing: they looked like old air-raid shelters, or escape tunnels for priests from the wrong church.

K had never thought before about where the water went after the world was finished with it or what might happen to it if it had nowhere to go. If, like language, it perpetuated itself. Or what would happen when there were no more holes left to fill. The grass already felt full up, sick of water. Was it possible that all the room for water was already used up? K knew that when they made the city, they had dug great lakes to allow for all the building over and filling in of holes, but what if they had built too much and not dug enough? What if there was more rain now? It seemed always to be snowing or raining. Was that just the time of year? Everything *was* getting greener; so maybe people had got it wrong again: the danger was not *to* the environment, but *from* the environment. People had spent so much time worrying about damaging the countryside that they had failed to notice how the countryside was conspiring to damage them, foxes and nettles creeping back into the city, tricking its architects into making great lakes and planting trees, soaking into lawns, covering paths and walls with moss and lichen, filling verges with spiky shrubs and jabbing saplings, some with eyes.

It was the square that calmed her.

Unlike the divisive procession of little trees either side of the path, here there was a simple, giant symmetry of huge tall things, somehow subservient, like infantry standing upright on parade, splendid but slaves. The square was not quite complete, the tyranny avoidable.

Which K found extra comforting. She had been worried by her own thoughts about geometry. Worried that the city might be a kind of lesson. The road grid was there, of course, but maybe there was a second grid: the primary inner grid of the roads around the big central buildings, and then a secondary outer grid, as if the whole symmetry had at some point breathed out and articulated a new thing through the roundabouts. If that was right, then it was not just Xscape that had an accumulative thing going on, but the whole city was an accumulation, a filling in of the gaps, and a filling up with rainwater and tears.

K began to wonder about the empty spaces she had felt... because, yes, she had *felt* them... around the back of Bannatynes and Argos, those creepy concrete pillars, that poignant road to nowhere, the tunnel she knew was probably just an entrance for delivery lorries but felt eerie, the huge mound that could have been where they reburied the bones of ancestors or just builders' spoil or a bunker where the old command centre had been abandoned after the planners gave up and the managers took over.

She was worried about what would happen when those areas of waste were filled in, that there would be an end of voids, that there would be nowhere to bury the hatchet and hide your feelings. Everything would be surface and shiny and revealed and her mission would be accomplished; a life's work, a very short one, complete. But what would happen to the feelings that were never satisfied? What was life for if not for moving on from?

Tied to a lamp post on the edge of the green was a waterlogged poster. It showed a picture of a youngish man of mixed race, dressed in a purple soccer strip and running, perfectly balanced, a model of dynamism. To K, not an enthusiast for the game, the colours meant nothing. There might have been a tree logo over the player's heart, but drops of rain had blurred the image. The poster called for "justice" for the guy; he had been "left at the coachway" at 2.02 in the morning. K had no appointment at the Coachway, she never used coaches, but she felt somehow compromised; she assumed that the call for justice meant that the man was dead. But how had he been "left"? Murdered and the body abandoned there? Dropped off still alive, but somehow "left"... to what? For what? Without what?

Being on the square allowed K to slide into things; it gave her a magical place, as if she could live forever on that flat surface, unreal and without dangers, the opposite to what she imagined abandonment at the Coachway might be like: the endless coming and going of the big machines, the queues of desperate people; only one rung up from refugees really. She suspected that homeless people were left at coachways, paid by the authorities in one town to move to another. And that the coaches were just an endless shuffling of homeless people and refugees from city to city.

It suddenly struck K that perhaps she could be arrested for thinking about things in the wrong way; and she ran away from the square. She had started to use things in inappropriate ways. She had not set out with that in mind, but now she was trying to get to her meetings by feeling her way, trying to recall the burnished map the city had given of itself, she had maybe been lured into too many compromising thoughts and actions, as now, climbing up the steps beside a children's slide, attracted by the tangle of silvery objects to swing from. There were no children about. On such a cold and potentially damp day it was unlikely any would be gathering any time soon to brave the chill of the metal, or the wetness soaking through their leggings from the slide. Even so, she made her way quickly to the top and kept going up the slope until she stood inside a dark gathering of conifers.

Under the trees it was dry and dusty. Grass had failed to take at the summit; shadowy yet lustrous, a satiny-look to the ground pleased her. It was something she wanted to be a part of, a meeting she realised she had always had an appointment for. No one came but the firs. She stood with them, feeling slightly uncomfortable. Their thick trunks were unthreatening, scarred and dignified. They might throw out a cape of green bravado to the world, but in their intimate club, they had their worries, their concerns for the planet, they were nervous about the prospects for their children, frightened by and about people. K felt their sadness seeping into the ground. It did not feed the roots, and K wondered where it would find to go. The trees invited her to touch them, and when she did they explained that they took almost all their thickness not from the ground, not from water in the soil, but from the air.

K felt a little giddy; partly from all the ideas that kept coming to her, as if the real matter of the city – the paths and trees and greens and lamp posts – was full of them, partly from the thought of speaking with trees, and partly from the height of the mound. All the time she was discovering new things to be frightened of.

K slithered down the fir tree mound and onto slippery grassiness, and then the full saturation again; the green here was more water than grass. For the first time, K began to fear for her shoes. She preferred comfortable to fashionable, for driving, but they were not walking boots. Was all the city this soaked through? On a rare patch of drier ground, someone had thrown down some kind of symbol, an awkward cross with two main crossbars and multiple spiky offshoots, across the top of which were three broken parts of a single piece of cream-coloured chipboard waiting for notices to be posted.

From the corner of Sutcliffe Ave. and Boycott Ave., bear right across another patch of grass with a huge square of trees. Cross the play area beyond the far line of trees, climb the steps to the slide, carrying on past the slide and up the slope to the small group of conifers on the top. Then go down the other side, bearing slightly right across another large patch of grass.

K made her way furtively down an alley between the houses; no one was following her, no sirens were sounded, no one appeared to have noticed that she was breaking all the rules she had made for herself. In fact, K was beginning to suspect that those rules were not all that she had cracked them up to be. Nor were roads and paths quite as simple and functional as she assumed. And alleys that she had always thought were places for ghosts and burglars were mainly occupied by sadnesses, surplus concrete and mattresses, cans and bags and other jilted packages.

This particular alley was even more sodden than the green squares! There were puzzling prints in the mud, as if a large snake had lain down to rest and been lifted away by hunters. An overflow pipe issued a constant stream of water and the side of the house was turning green. There was a frame that might once have housed something, but its single trail of ivy was like a signature on a blank painting.

> Take the alleyway ahead, running between back gardens and houses and then crossing Hutton Avenue, running along the backs of the houses (with a kink in the middle) through Verity Place to Oldbrook Blvd.

The airy boulevard closed in tighter than the alleyway. K's priorities were being changed by her circumstances; where she would have felt safety, she now experienced exposure, as if the passing cars might suddenly reverse up, allowing a crowd of passengers to disembark and ask her exactly what she had discussed in her meeting with the firs. But there were no minutes of the meeting! She felt inside her pocket, but her phone was gone, back in the car of course. It was too late to turn back and break the window now. She had a biro and a tiny notepad taken from a hotel. She tried to write a heading in shorthand but she did not know any, so she copied the graffiti under the flyover:

SORRY WORLD

Climbing the broken steps was like entering an archaeological site. The city was not a futuristic place, but more ancient, where water and trees were patiently waiting to re-establish the wetness they had lost. She suspected that the Sun was involved, pulling strings in the background; not necessarily in a good way.

The moss was as thick as a good carpet on part of the path; someone had dropped a pot of pink emulsion, which had hardened into the fossil remains of something with a large skull and a long tail that walked upright. The two mounds on either side of the V road, their undergrowth thrashed back to bareness, afforded a view to the dome of Christ the Cornerstone from one mound and to the hemisphere of Xscape from the other. It was a clever trick: shaping the vantage points the same as the things that could be seen from them. It connected what you were to what there was. K felt rooted in the mounds.

Crossing the bridge, K had noticed that the smell of the rat and her empathy for the homeless person were following in her shadow, and she drove them away with threats. On the second dome-like mound she found a broken part of a vacuum cleaner, or something like that, but it might also have been a toy model of something Luke Skywalker flew.

K climbed down from the planners' dirty joke. Or perhaps they were fake pre-history, giving the ancient landscape a helpful nudge: all history was a fake, of course, the past was gone and what bits remained were only distinguished by their different levels of unreliability. Old didn't mean real. That's why people were more frightened of ghosts than they were frightened of history; everyone can see that history depends too much on what you believe about it already. Ghosts, however, make you scared no matter what you think. K was worried that she was starting to lose her drift. Like the square, the double curved lines of the trees were calming; domes again.

Turn left up Oldbrook Boulevard, crossing the end of Larwood Place, and before reaching the underpass cross right across Oldbrook Boulevard and up the steps on the other side and then up the path to the edge of Saxon Street, turning right along the Redway parallel with Saxon Street. Go past the bus stop, following the Redway that bears to the right and up to a mound on the right-hand side of the path. Climb the mound, then come back down and take the bridge over Saxon Street signposted to Fishermead, then climb the mound on the other side, come back down and take the Redway running parallel with Chaffron Way (in the same direction as when you were crossing the bridge). After passing a small section of low brick wall on your right, on the left is a grass space marked out by circles of tall thin trees; go to the middle, marked out by shrubs, which has a small secluded space within it which is linked by a path from the houses.

The whole city is a ritual space without any rituals, she thought. Well, maybe there are rituals in a chapel here and there, and in the bedrooms of a handful of enthusiasts; sport has its rituals, but nowhere near enough to fill all the waiting sacred spaces in MK. K stood in the launch pad, whatever it was supposed to be... and her situation became blindingly clear to her... the map she had been given was not the map to her meetings.

There were three grids in her vision. The first was the traffic system. The second was the wobbly five pointed star that would take her to all her pitches. The third was the shape of the soul of the city itself; K could not think of a better word than 'soul'. It wasn't just atmosphere or feeling, there was a shape – like ghosts have a shape, like in churches souls are depicted as babies with wings, sometimes just the heads and wings – those were souls... and symmetries like the cylinder brain – these were ideas transcending goodness, but they all have shapes... well, that was what the third grid was and that was what K had to walk.

If she... managed to make her pitches... well... maybe she would not get fired, but first she had to save the soul shape of the city; only then could she save her job... the usual priorities...

> Return to the Redway parallel with Chaffron Way and continue in the same direction. The path begins to climb and on your left is a 'den' just within the trees.

The city was much, much richer than she had imagined. The distractions from her destination were beginning to worry her; she had expected to slide across empty and neutral spaces, but despite all the aching ritual voids she had found, there were also all these spiky and particular places, like the concrete platform, the slide, the grabbing bramble and the road to nowhere. K was following the crazy-paving path of a den through a tight thicket of small trees to an inner sanctum, which, in a neat organisational irony that appealed to K, was also at the outer edge of the trees. This exposed sanctuary, hiding in plain sight, had its own one-armed throne, a fence of sticks and a floor pattern: a square within a square, the inner square of which – with small rectangular spars – aligned to create triangles. The same kind of twist in orientation that K had felt when she ran from the ceremonial path with the honour guard of trees; perhaps the den was a place of initiation for those leaving the grid for a while.

It was the start of the school day and parents were milling about the local centre. Children were directed and corralled through a wedge-shaped gap between the fish bar and the supermarket. K stayed light on her feet, dodging around the families coming and going; she felt nervous around children and families. Her childlessness made her somehow suspect among kids and parents, she felt; they might think she was a baby farmer. She hurried through the brick complex of shops, pub and school, head down. She barely glimpsed Eagles Jerk & Grill, its bright yellow interior throbbing like a Kodachrome sunrise, three smiling young black men draped around the order counter, one in a rastacap. If she had looked more carefully she might not have missed the convocation of superheroes stood at the back of the shop. A seven-foot rat stood on hind legs, a female tour guide, an archangel, a fairy with an odour problem, an androgynous figure dressed in black and wearing opaque goggles and an almost unnoticeable pair of legs in working trousers were gathered around a brightly coloured if ragged Triceratops who was berating a stone.

"Look, mate", yelled the Triceratops, prodding the air with his horny trident for emphasis, "you've got your head up where the sun don't shine no more, the planners were idiots, there was no plan!"

"Pardon me" said the stone, firmly, "I was speaking..."

"Get on with it" urged the rat. The figure in the goggles drew more deeply into the corner of the shop.

The stone cleared its throat.

"I'm not saying there's a plan..."

"You bloody were just now" roared the dinosaur, "why can't you make up your mind!"

"Once I make up my mind, it doesn't change for millennia; one has to be wary of such rashness, that way earthquakes lie..."

"Perhaps", interposed the guide, "we could agree that whether there is or is not a plan... and I think Bill", she nodded at the Triceratops, "means that there is no good or workable plan rather than no plan at all, well, whatever, perhaps we could agree..."

"Spit it out, woman" prodded the dinosaur, thumping a giant-toed foot on the restaurant's tiles.

"...plan or not, there is the appearance of a plan..."

"Jesus Christ on a stick!" yelled the rat in frustration, causing the legs to shuffle nervously, and the three men at the counter to briefly turn inquisitively. "We don't have to agree exactly what we want to protect, we just need to protect it. We need to pool our powers..."

"What powers exactly does that thing 'ave?"

The Triceratops tilted his horns at the black-clad figure and the archangel suddenly expanded its wings until they filled the whole of the ceiling of Eagles Jerk & Grill.

"You do not see as I see", said the archangel in a high-pitched voice, the shadowy figure in goggles moving in elegant shapes to the music of his words. "Among the living there is a weakness for flesh and a weakness for the destruction, rejection and transcendence of flesh. Some who cannot live easily in their bodies seek escape, by their own volition or in general projects by which they seek to drag down or burn up the community of their fellows. I think such a business is beginning again, and in the interests of flesh..."

"Hold yer 'orses, ain't you a spirit?"

The archangel glared at the Triceratops, his eyes like burning coals, yet his voice remained cool and soft.

"Lucifer was an angel. All of us who no longer walk the earth, but are condemned to fly or creep or hide, suffer for the loss of our imperfect materials. 'Be careful what you pray for...' they say. If only we had listened! Let us combine our powers and talents to save the living Miltonians from destroying the one thing worth having in this city..."

"Mud!" roared the Triceratops. "Fat", sniggered the rat. "Fertiliser", sang the woman guide. The black-clad figure mimed closing a door on himself. "Faeces", agreed the fairy. "Bricks... er... or, no, not bricks", bumbled the erratic, "statues, sculptures, no, no, I go back to bricks..."

"Exactly", whistled the archangel, "exactly."

The legs danced a little jig, for they knew now that whether or not it was a plan they were protecting, or simply a jumble of things, or at worst the appearance of either, they were once more an assembly of heroes ready to save the city from itself. Grabbing their bagged portions of BBQ belly pork, jerk chicken wings and callaloo and cabbage stew, the superheroes left the shop, disappearing into a mixture of spirit, tiny creeping thing, shadow, grit and unprepossessing passer-by that split to the five corners of the city, leaving a furious Bill to pick up the bill.

Carry on along the Redway and cross the bridge on the right over Chaffron Way. Go down the steps on the other side, crossing Harrier Drive, walk between the two yellow posts and into Eaglestone local centre, past the Premier shop, turning to the left, passing Falconhurst School on your right. Turn right up High Trees; then up the steps on your left and bear right past garages on your left and go through the metal barriers into the alleyway signed 'High Trees' and 'North Ridge'. Go around a circular shrub bed and carry straight on out the other side, following the path ahead to a road area with garages directly to your left. The road (North Ridge) forms a kind of square with trees in the middle; go straight across this 'square' and take the alleyway on the far side. At the next junction of paths turn right, and at the following junction of paths turn left. This soon brings you out on a grass space beside Harrier Drive.

Following Ferndale and coming out onto Harrier Drive, unnerved by a feeling of alienation from the community of yelling and joyous kids and upbraiding and joking parents, K was soothed by the sight of a fairy ring in the grass. Five trees stood around it; as if in a meeting with it, reminding K of the star she was following. The thicker grass that formed the ring had grown that way because somewhere in the centre of the circle, probably some years before, a single spore of fungus had fallen and from it, evenly in all directions, an underground network of tube-like threads had wormed outwards and absorbed all the nutrients from the ground, pushing up new mushrooms and fertilising the grass, until that network had used up all the goodness, first in the centre and then later further out, and so the network slowly died out, until only a ring at its edge survived, fuelling extra growth, until that, eventually, disappeared.

"Or fairies made it", said a smelly thought. K hurried on.

Cross Harrier Drive where the path with two concrete bollards meets the road; follow this path on the other side of Harrier Drive towards Marlborough St., take the path as it turns into steps down to the right, then turn right along the Redway, through the underpass signed 'Peartree Bridge'.

Follow the footpath straight ahead, and bear right into Waterside which bends around to the right, the Grand Union Canal immediately on your left. Take the first bridge over the canal on your left, then drop down the steps beside the bridge on your left and turn left along the tow path (same direction along the canal as before). Just before the next bridge slip through the gap in the hedge on your left, turn right over the canal bridge and then turn left along Waterside with the canal now on your left. Further down Waterside turn right through the white railings.

Inorganic, and every bit as elegant as the Ferndale fairy ring, were the four blank information boards on a small path to a play area and the remnant of an old orchard. Just beyond the four boards, which were raised on silver poles, two either side of the path in a trapezoid (a sloping rectangle in two dimensions, suggestive of a decapitated pyramid in three dimensions), the footpath forked in a Y shape; branching out in response to the poled boards squeezing in. The blank grey boards were a little bigger than sheets of A4; on their reverse sides the first two boards were decorated with swirling labyrinths of glue that had once affixed notices; each began at the edges of the board as a rectangle and then turned ovular in the centre, one with a vertical eye-shape in the middle, the other with a horizontal one. As K made her way along the backs of the gardens, skirting a dead rat, she began to wonder if there was some pattern to all the patterns, that if she could correctly arrange the fairy ring, the glue labyrinth, the two mounds, the domes, the malevolent guarded path and all the rest, she might come to an answer that could cancel the question of the city.

Lumbering across the green towards K, the Triceratops was battered and wounded, the wire mesh of its innards exposed beneath its tattoos of bright paint. It had arrow slits for eyes. K had caught it staring at the traffic on the V8, its massive mostly green body turned towards her, but its head hidden by a purple frill around its neck. K had tried to step quietly along the pavement, using the cover afforded by two lamp posts, but the huge head had swivelled, slowly and theatrically, as if the beast knew all along that she was there. Gleefully and momentarily, the Triceratops ogled her with reptilian eyes, then tore itself from its concrete plinth and loped towards her, shaking the pavement beneath her feet. K, frozen with fear, rooted to the tarmac, was already flinching from the strike of its horny trident when the dinosaur pulled up.

Its voice was wild and woolly.

"By popular request, following my latest failure, ha ha ha! Run, the police are after me!! 'Where's your license to be prehistoric, mate!?!' This city needs things like me, the planners are idiots!!! The roof of our cave fell in on our bed the other night! I wanna blow more than a few raspberries at the planners!"

And he let loose a monstrous fart that made the lamp posts twitch and an SUV swerve on Marlborough Street; there was something prehistoric and horrific about the smell, as if an era died and went bad, but there was also a smell of damp plaster and dried paint. K noticed how blotchy the face of the behemoth was; despite its bulk and the sinister slits of its snaky eyes, the pinks and limes gave it the look of a big squeaky toy. Chunks of material had fallen from its neck scallops and exposed the slats and wires of its primitive infrastructure.

"You are hardly in the best position to lecture anyone about architecture!"

When in a fix, K thought, fire first; though her body was trembling involuntarily and violently.

"Cheeky bloody monkey", said the Triceratops. "What do you want – my last will and testament? Send my front door to the British Museum and let the tourists weep! I'll 'ave you for breakfast before you bury my ashes under Wavendon Tower!"

"But you're a vegetarian."

"So what? You scamp, I'll skewer you with me postorbital horn cores!"

And the Triceratops performed a combat roll, leaping into a soft style fighting stance. K's voice shook as she spoke; she sounded to herself like a bad connection or a singer with hiccups using a vocoder.

"The latest research s...s...uggests that your horns were not used for fighting, not even for defending yourself, but for identification and c..courtship."

"Oh", said the Triceratops, "fancy a snog, then?"

"No, thank you."

"Don't let 'em get rid of me!" The dinosaur was on its knees, the tips of its horns picking out the soft tissue in K's torso. It was easier not to fear the dinosaur in theory than in practice. "They're always threatening to. They let me fall apart so they can say I'm an eyesore, they say I'm crude, or a danger to public 'ealth, don't let 'em bury me in Milton Keynes, will you, love? I don't wanna become 'ardcore on a building site! All them little boxes, lonely units of isolation all 'round me, no one communicatin'... whose gonna 'old a séance for a Triceratops? Thing o' me, darlin', thing o' me, don't let them trash me..."

The Triceratops got up, in an ungainly manner, and stood on its back legs. It seemed to blot out the sky, its centre horn piercing the middle of a weak Sun, it looked like a demon; the animal, for all its crudity and homely vernacular, had a fearless authority that K had never faced, not even in boardrooms. This thing had survived T Rex; what had she survived? A tribunal? Sarcasm?

"... you know they're still telling lies about me... they make 'em up in that black propaganda studio they've had up there for years..."

What was he talking about?

"...don't let them blight my memory... I never 'ad permission to exist in the first place so there ain't no authority on earth as can give permission for me to be destroyed... saving an asteroid, p'raps... "

Without moving, it was back on its plinth; without turning, it was back to watching the traffic on the V8. Rattled in her guts and her limbs shivering with fright, K turned and ran incoherently up the footpath towards the canal, jumping sideways at the sight of a giant concrete bunny in the garden of the big house! Tripping over her own feet, K performed a graceful forward lunge before regaining her momentum, quickly turning her back on a kind of rough thinking that she dismissed to herself as primeval and superseded.

"Put a different dinosaur on every roundabout, people'll know where they are then... 'turn left at the T Rex' and 'straight on at the Plesiosaur'..."

The long-haired voice faded as K strode, her mind agitated, her body shaking all over, to the bridge across the Grand Union Canal. She put both hands on the bridge and leaned over the water, stealing from its calmness; in the flat surface of the canal was the reflection of an amputated arm sat on a green-wrapped anvil shape at the edge of the water. She was relieved when she looked directly at it; it was made of plaster, but even so. Two tears in a bucket! The city was dancing on her nerves right now and the people in Fox Milne were depending on her!

Turn left at the small play area and follow the path along the backs of the gardens, straight on through the play area at the end of the path and turn right along Waterside as it then turns sharply to the left.

~#~

Suggested end point for Walk 1: Bill Billings Triceratops sculpture, between Waterside and Marlborough Street.

Walk 2

Suggested start point: Bill Billings Triceratops sculpture, between Waterside and Marlborough Street

Estimated walking time: 2 hours

From the Bill Billings Triceratops sculpture,
between Waterside and Marlborough Street,
walk to Waterside taking the footpath running
beside the Old Rectory Farm, passing
between two metal bollards.

Much, much weirder than the play paint dinosaur or the pale plaster amputation, the Green was like the set for a scary old TV play or an early colour Dr Who – K had dated a nerdish guy once who made her sit through endless things like that, TV Christmas ghost plays on dvd, the kind where something very old was dug up (usually something to do with the devil and that later turned out to be a front for something worse or it was something else that turned out to be a front for the devil), set in a place, usually a village, where old stones and mounds had ideas of their own and the locals were scared of certain names and places. There would be possessed Morris dancers, dogs with glowing eyes and scientists would arrive with computers and the ancient would speak back to the software. K scanned the edges of the Green for any sign of rampaging prehistoric monsters, but there was a different kind of foreboding here; an English eeriness. There was something about the wide expanse of green, the way the road turned and its progress after that was hidden, how there was no distinction between roadway and grass platform, only a continuation of flatness; the space had a heldness, a potency that K could feel reach out to her.

The information board explained the strange shape of the village: the huge village green at the centre, houses built around the edges. It had developed during the 1600s. For reasons no one had found fit to record or remember, people had abandoned their homes in the centre and built around the edges, allowing the buildings in the centre to go to ruin.

The village had turned itself inside out and reassembled on the green, grass growing up through the buildings in the middle. Woughton was like a giant fairy ring, but of human fungi. K imagined the same thing happening to MK: the central grid abandoned and the suburbs expanding while the big structures in the middle collapsed, the green rising up through its bones. What kind of spawn could cause that? What had fallen in the middle of Woughton all those years before? Plague? Flood? A witch hunt? Something powerful enough to hollow out the nourishment at the heart of its community, bringing its architecture to the ground? Did kids dare each other to visit the ruins at night? Did builders steal materials from the old village or were they scared of transferring the curse to new homes? Did the death of a heart turn a human into faerie?

K tried the handle of the church door, but it was locked.

> Take the bridge over the Canal and follow the path ahead as it joins the road across The Green. Go between the white fences on the other side. Follow this road (The Green) to the junction with Newport Rd. (Ye Olde Swan pub is on your right). Bear left, cross Newport Rd. to St Mary's Church, enter through the lych gate.

She took an old corpse path. She had imagined the grass and woody verges along the edges of the transport grid were just that: verges. But they were not; their green ran inwards from the grid for what seemed like miles; a whole other countryside was hidden *inside* the city. The shapes were just one platform, the green was another, and there might be many others, but the gaze of the grey slug monster would fall upon them all.

Walk down the right side of the church, through the graveyard to a gap in the wall on the right. Once through the gap, turn left and follow the footpath behind the houses and then under the trees, until straight ahead of you is blocked and there is a gate on your left. Go through this into open green space. Where the paths fork, take the right fork, with a distant view to Xscape to your left.

Take the raised wooden walkway, then pass a pond on your right and go through a group of trees; at the next junction of paths take the second left, then straight on at the following junction of paths and walk with the River Ouzel on your right. Take the bridge across the river and follow the path signed to 'Oakgrove' passing under Chaffron Way then around to the right. Now cross the bridge over the river, with a ford on your left, follow the path round to the left then bend to the right and uphill, ignoring the "Private land: no public access" sign to the right, and go over the raised wooden walkway.

Turn right along Harvard Way, cross the road, then turn left down Hanson Ave. At Babbage Gate turn in left along the front of the Metro Bank and then across the square, passing between Pets Corner and Waitrose.

K stopped off at Costa for a flat white. The shiny new shops and the family playing badminton on the square had filled her with dread; whenever she was asked to pitch to corporations outside the city, or even to ones based here, if she was asked to sum up or describe MK, she had in her mind certain stereotypes; of steel and concrete and glass utopia, of dystopian order and regimentation, of knowing how carefully angled those images were that they put up in Centre:MK. On foot, there was neither utopia nor dystopia, but there was still the angle, because K was beginning to realise that she was a camera, that she was creating a city for herself by walking it and part of it was the landscape at Woughton on the Green: the idea that these centres could one day lie hollow and abandoned. Even the mid shot of the amputated arm and the close up of the enigmatic piece of trash on the mound. Could some kind of spawn or depression eat the heart out of here?

K paid for her coffee at the counter, took it over to a table, and – just in case she was not going to pass anywhere for a while (she refused to go squatting in shrubs) – she decided to use Costa's loo. There was nothing to indicate if the toilet was in use or not. "Do I need a code?" she asked the assistant. She did not. Opening the door very slightly, K peered diplomatically through the smallest of cracks, and glimpsed that there was already someone in there. Before she could close the door, the figure turned around and K screamed at the sight of the black material that wrapped it entirely, the face shrouded and the smoked glass goggles that covered its eyes. It reached out protectively to K with two gloved hands. She turned and ran out of the shop without touching her coffee.

On the far side of the square (at Costa) turn right down Atlas Way, then left down Aiken Grange following the road as it turns to the left, then take the path on your right (with ponds immediately on your left) and follow this path under Brickhill St. At the crossroads of paths go straight on, past the small stone pyramid (with a missing top) in the middle of the path, past the sign to 'Middleton Park'.

Speeding under Brickhill Street, K paused at the trapezoidal concrete bollard and spun around, expecting the black-shrouded figure to be in her face. She scoured the underside of the road bridge for any sign that she had been shadowed, checked the small trees either side of the path for signs of abrasive dinosaurs. Again, nothing. A church tower ahead did the work of the grey slug, scanning the inner and absent heart of the city; was that the nature of the dark thing? The absence where the heart had been? In what, in who, in her? Surely, not. It was necessary to be tough in business; not heartless. K would meet her obligations no matter what the day threw at her. She went to check the time on her phone – she could have asked at the coffee shop – but, of course, it was still in her car. A small mistake and there was no safety net of public time to catch her. She noted that such soft viciousness was only evident in the event of small accidents; they must build that into the pitch. The feeling grid that K had devised would seek out those who tripped, who were lost, had forgotten their mission, and would draw them all into its embrace.

The door of the church was locked. Two churches tried, two churches locked. These were buildings of the Church of

England! K shouted at the recalcitrant door. "I am English! Partly... How dare you lock me out! Christ on a cracker!"

She hammered on the door. She had not been inside a church for years, but she believed in a God of some kind. It stood to reason. Someone or some *thing* must have been sitting on the wrong side of the Big Bang when it went off; blew them so far back folk had been praying for them to return ever since. It was a homespun mystery, easier to cope with than all that crap about dinosaurs and sacrifices and whatever in the hell was motivating the people who had been mutilating cats and dogs and horses according to the posters on the lamp posts. What kind of god were they worshipping?

Someone had left an Amazon parcel in the front porch; presumably for the vicar, but when K checked the address it was for somewhere on the other side of town. K could deliver it, she was going that way. There was a human need to believe in something bigger than money. On her way out of the churchyard gate she paused to read the sparkly new gravestone for the Saxons.

God, Milton Keynes was so old!

At the junction of paths take the left-hand path (with the view to a church tower). Turn right at a T-junction of paths (as you approach there is a stone pyramid on your right) along a path signed 'Milton Keynes Village' with a church wall to the left of the path. Turn right into Willen Rd., follow it around to the left past the Swan Inn, turn left into Broughton Rd. and immediately left again into the narrow footpath along the far side of the brick bus shelter.

Follow this path between the hedges, then
bear left into a small paved public garden
area and out the other side winding to the
left and right through the cottages until you
come to a green space with the Village Hall
straight ahead. Bear left to the far left
corner of the green space and the junction
of Willen Road and Great Pasture, cross the
road to the church, go through the gate,
enter All Saints churchyard.

Back in the middle of the village, Milton Keynes Village
now – presumably they added the 'Village' after they built
the city round it? – she had jumped for joy at the sight of
an old red public phone box. More pink than red, burnt in
the malicious Sun. Now she could phone ahead, warn them
at Fox Milne, the operator could patch her through… were
there still operators? Problem was, there was no phone; the
box was a shell, a white cord hung down from where the
machine had been. A sign to say that ownership had been
transferred from British Telecom. K let the heavy door shut
behind her. She stared out, like a prisoner, between the bars
of the windows. This was how everywhere would be soon;
the engineers would arrive not to install machines but to
remove them. Nanotechnology would operate at the level
of dust, information would be gathered emotionally by
tripping quantum super-positions, there would be no
intrusion of privacy because there would be no privacy,
everything would be connected, as it really was. They were
bringing back God from beyond the event horizon. She
laughed and her hilarity echoed harshly in the enclosed
space. Soon, there would be no more old.

The engraving said the remains of 100 Saxons were buried there. Under such a small stone. It would have been much better to bury them under that huge mound next to the Argos offices in town. A quotation from the Book of Ezekiel on the stone: "he asked me 'son of man, can these bones live?'" What K might have realised, if she had been inside a church more often, was that the passage ran on "behold, I will cause breath to enter you... I will put sinews on you, make flesh grow back on you, cover you with skin and put breath in you that you may come alive..."

Beneath the stone, there was movement.

"Excuse me?"

K span round.

No shadow, no living corpse, no angry fossil; a young man in an Amazon uniform.

"Do you know this?"

He held up a hand-held GPS device and a parcel. The address bore no relation to the marker on the screen. K held up her parcel.

"Did you just deliver this to the church?"

"Yes."

"It's nowhere near here, it's for Bradwell..."

"Ale jaja! I'm sorry..."

And he took the parcel from K and stared at the address.

"O Jezu!"

He shook the GPS device. A pizza van drew up, a liveried man with a long black beard got out and the two deliverymen began to converse sheepishly in a conflation of languages from a fairytale Mittel-Europa, like two small children abandoned in the Grimm forest of modern England. K left them to their own devices. She had the good news of her own gospel to deliver.

A green woodpecker took off, flashing the bright yellow stripe of its back, and K followed the arc of its flight into the tops of the tall pines.

Come out of the churchyard by the same gate and then turn left along Willen Rd., until it reaches a fork. Take the Redway path, which is the left-hand route, leaving Willen Rd. which turns to the right, and follow this Redway path until you see a blue Public Footpath sign on your left. Take this small dirt track behind the houses and through the trees until you see a gap in the wooden fence to your right and take that. Now turn left along Noon Layer Drive, crossing the end of Wolston Meadow, then turn left along the path into Middleton Park (sign on left of the path).

Where the path forks, take the right-hand fork and go past the medieval fish pond on your left, until you see the Redway up ahead of you. Bear right across the grass and then turn right along this Redway, crossing Noon Layer Drive into Oak Valley Park (there is a sign to the right of path). Follow this path, passing a play area to your right, until you reach a junction of paths and take the path straight on signposted to Ouzel Valley Park – South and Willen Lake.

No one would buy the Swan. The Swan assumed this could only be because He was divine, indeed, that He was the most powerful divine thing there was. He was the Gift, the God King, the Father God, the Authorised Seducer, the Hammer of the Weak and the Exploiter of the Fruits. More than that, He was a spiritual icon, "oh, you're a Work of Art, you are!" A suitable subject for a family park, He was a hybrid of animal/hand/woman, a divine magus and His neck was an unfolding thunderbolt, unnoticed between the sweets stall and the Apple Core Carousel.

K had arrived at the Lake under the calming and pillared thickness of the Childs Way flyover and had been marvelling at the line of lycra joggers who dropped to their hands and knees and were performing press ups. At the feet of their trainer sat a collection of antiquarian weights, in measures of pounds and ounces, as if these rituals had been performed lakeside for decades, maybe longer, urgently warding off an encroaching something that was collectively feared.

K had checked for shadows in 'The Lakeside' before using their toilets. Outside again, she watched as a flotilla of swans paraded across the water. White swan-pedalos churned among pink and green dragons.

"I am the Father of Aphrodite!"

K looked around. None of the joggers had broken their star jumps. She stared at their trainer; it was an unusual instruction.

"The children of other men address *me* as Father!"

There was an ear-splitting crack. From over by the sweets stall, shards of granite spat across the path, a few made trails of spume in the lake itself. There were gasps of delight. Children examined their ice cream cones; adults turned to each other. The Sun blazed.

"My father tried to eat me, but he sucked a stone!"

The sweets stall holder checked his wares.

A woman broke in pieces. The fingers of a giant hand fell one by one apart and broke on the lakeside pavement. A maid in the Premier Inn glanced out of the window and then continued with her cleaning.

"I command the waters of the lake to rise and drown the human race! I will remake the people in stone, more ready for the hardness of life!"

The pink and green pedalos continued to churn around each other; the swans cruised by, the level of the water was unchanged.

"Βάλλ εἰς κόρακας!" went roaring across the water in ancient Greek, but that had no effect either.

From the centre of the granite fragments a stone Swan rose up, a chain of granite swinging from His neck.

"You like my chain, sweet one?" The Swan was speaking directly to K now. "It symbolises the chain of life, in which we are all imprisoned. 'We are all just prisoners here, of our own device'. My favourite band – The Swans."

"The Eagles", K corrected.

"μά τὸν κύνα! We got a live one here! O baby!"

The Swan padded round on His giant feet and the paving cracked beneath His granite waders. The Swan thrust out His chest and opened His wings like a clothes horse draped with marble linen. The final pieces of ruined art fell to the path.

"I got to find the passage back to where I was before. You're a very attractive young woman, you know? Can I share your highway? Hahaha!"

"What are you?"

The stone Swan pointed the tip of His right wing to the corner of His left eye and winked; and when the lid re-opened the Sun shone out and dazzled and blinded K so that she staggered backwards.

"I'm a real bobby-dazzler! You can stab Me with your steely knives, but you just can't kill *this* Beast! Hahaha!"

K felt a stone sheet descending over her and she pushed back. She could still see nothing, but she could feel the claustrophobic granite assault. She kicked with her feet and punched and slapped with her hands and her vision began to clear.

"Resistance is futile!" said the stone Swan in a fake German accent, His long white neck reaching up to the sky in a salute to the malignant Sun. K seized her chance. She kicked the Swan's legs from under Him and for a comical moment He rose up on a flurry of stony down before hammering into the ground in a dry belly flop. He pulled Himself out of the crater made by His fall and raised the giant sails of His wings, racing after K down the lakeside path at full speed, past the empty tracks of the miniature railway, past the watchtower-like structures of the tree top adventure facility. The two of them ducked under the H6, leaping the train tracks one after the other, then reeling off the path and into the long grass around the tall trunks of the Pine Plantation.

The path signposted to Ouzel Valley Park –
South and Willen Lake swings round to the
left, following the river; turn right across
the footbridge over the river and take the
path straight ahead under the dual flyover
carrying Childs Way and take the path,
going to the left with the lake on your
right-hand side, and passing the Aerial
Extreme site on your left. Follow the path
around the edge of the lake (the lake on
your right) and pass the Freedom Leisure
and Premier Inn buildings on your left until
you reach the 'Leda and the Swan'
sculpture.

~#~

Suggested end point for Walk 2: Leda and
Swan sculpture, next to Premier Inn and
'The Lakeside' Restaurant, Willen Lake.

Walk 3

Suggested start point: Leda and Swan sculpture, next to Premier Inn and 'The Lakeside' Restaurant, Willen Lake

Estimated walking time: 3 hours

> From the Leda and Swan sculpture, take the path beside the lake, with the lake on your left. After you pass Aerial Extreme on your right, turn right under the Childs Way flyover and then turn left into the trees.

Deftly, K jumped behind one of the trees. The stone Swan was momentarily flummoxed by her disappearance. He was not a hunting bird. It was a stupid guise for an abusive god. Even craning His long neck He could barely see around a single trunk at a time. Meanwhile, K was skilfully moving from tree to tree, careful to make as little noise as possible. The Swan King stalked the lines of pines like a guard patrolling prison blocks.

"διαρραγείης!" He yelled to K, in frustration. This was no way for a King, the Star of the Heavens, to be treated; what had possessed that κύων to cast Him, the Sun, in stone? In light and fire He would have had this female by now; but the night was already falling and He felt His power draining into the roots of the trees.

K flitted from trunk to trunk. She never allowed a glimpse of her to escape to the Swan. Nevertheless, in the subsequent hours of growing terror, caught in a game she could not end, she began to feel worn down. Trapped in a nightmare of her own device, she knew there was no Swan, there was no King, there was no Sun cast in granite trying to catch her; she knew that the perception of crime was always far, far greater than the reality. Yet this was one Beast she could not kill with information.

The Sun reflected on its situation; oh, yes, of course the politically-correct snowflakes-gone-mad would all be howling bonkers because He had had the temerity to express His own designs. Wasn't she beautiful? In the name of Zeus! They could all throw themselves to the crows, nobody was going to tell Him that she wasn't working her wiles; she was calling on Aphrodite, his own daughter, for the love of a sack of wine!

No matter how much K told herself the threat was in her own mind, she could not bring herself to step from behind the trunk. After a while she had stopped switching between the trees and allowed the Swan to waste His energy bumbling along the rows, in the hope that He would exhaust Himself. But He would not give in. Evening closed in and her Fox Milne meeting was long ago ended. K's mind drifted to her pitch; if there was no real Swan, no genuine threat, would her cordless, wireless, machineless sensibility system generate one if just from the fear of Him? Everyone knew a Swan could break a person's heart with one flap of His wing...

No, no...

She woke from her reverie to see the stone-faced Swan Thing a few metres away, backing around a pine and turning His beak towards her; even in the gloom she saw the whiteness of the gleam of His hard plumage. There was no time for her to step back behind a trunk or move to another hiding place; the Swan was too close, and He was moving closer, head erect, chest tumescent.

Then the Swan was gone.

Then the female was gone.

A darkness fell across the part of the Pine Plantation where the predatory god had been flapping towards her.

She had just vanished into the thin air leaving only a dark smear where she had stood a moment before.

K stood stock still. She had no idea what had just happened, but she felt something else was very close and she should not move. But when did she ever do as she should? She tried to tip toe to the nearest tree; as she did the darkness between her and the Swan mimicked her movements. K froze, the darkness froze; a void in the shape of her own figure was all that stood between her and the Swan a few centimetres away, a thin defence made of shadow and loneliness. After a while she heard the Swan crash through the long grass nearer the lake, then the crunch of His granite palmate feet slapping the path towards Aerial Extreme. K shifted her weight in an effort to see. For a moment, it was like looking around the edge of night. Quickly, she leaned back into the darkness, then leaned forward again into the grey evening glow. The abusive god was disappearing under the concrete flyover, back towards His plinth. K took her chance, sprinting through the trees parallel with the lakeside, in the opposite direction to the Swan, her muscles screaming with stiffness. She looked back only once, fearing she might trip. There was no stone Thing, but where she had been hiding there was darkness in the shape of a figure. It turned towards her and there was a twin glint of street light in the lenses of a pair of goggles, then its nothingness blended into the gloom and was indistinguishable from the rest of the plantation. K kept running.

Up and to K's left, vans, lorries and cars were racing along the raised roadway, their beams spilling into the plantation. The grass was long and wet. It soaked the trousers of K's suit.

Light. K had never thought about light before. In the sense of noticing, really noticing. Yes, of course, she saw light and shadow, she knew when she could see and when things got dim; but this was different. Before now, light to her was just a function of seeing – a question of was there enough to see or not? – but now light was an agent in itself, light did things, made things happen, or the lack of it closed things down. Light scared K. Crossing under the double-bridge carrying Childs Way, there was an eeriness about the spills of headlight beams that flickered on the water and threw up a rectangle of wriggling reflections on the underside of the bridge, like a badly tuned thought-movie.

> **Walk through the trees, going parallel with the road until you get to the path with the River Ouzel beyond it.**

It was a relief to K to be scrabbling up the steep bank of grass, her feet slipping in the wet, just to feel her muscles pushing away the distortion of her thoughts. The lake was close. Swans were close. Get away. Even the lights along Childs Way gave her a temporary feeling of safety, running under the big road sign felt like she was achieving something, even if she had no idea what her goal was any more. Shell. Holiday Inn. Their signs hung in the air like uprooted ghosts. The Shell sign was just a shell. And who went to a Holiday Inn on holiday? Words and things were being pushed apart. And when that happened what was there to think with? Symmetries? The vicious rectangle of the dark underpass? Even that shape was preferable to the granite-hard plumage of the Swan.

The street lamps along the road were a kind of comfort. Tiny white flowers, daisies, were picked out around her feet by sodium light. There were no real stars that K could see. The stars were all in the ground. She trod on one or two; extinguished the odd galaxy. There were sliding flat planes; reflections on the bodies of ponds. In the weak light of the lamps she was drawn to an information board; it was some bleeding-heart wildlife blather about nesting swans. Bomb 'em all.

K wanted to break away from the road, but the footpath on the right, lined with regimental trees, was too like the ritual path she had run from earlier in the day. That's what this was all about, right? A routine that K refused to be part of? Why else would anyone be afraid of trees?

K was surprised by the young black guy leaning into the hedge, waiting for something, Red Stripe in hand. He was cool. K was waiting too, but she could only wait by moving; if she stopped, leaned back like that, everything would catch her up. There were things that were only waiting for her to pause, then they would pounce. She would have loved to lean back with that guy and drink Red Stripe together.

A perverted pyramid. A triangle shaped like a fang. Or a wishbone. K could not care less that the bridge might be her quickest, brightest, safest way. It might even be some kind of escape pod, or portal to a happy arrival back home, or the gatehouse to an armed citadel where she would be secure. It even looked like all that. But none of that held; it was poisoned geometry. K had no idea why, but it was poisoned, and she was sure she would learn eventually. She was in a hurry to know, right now.

She cut left down the footpath, with the brook to her right. The path got darker and darker. The ominous gatherings of bushes and trees around the grass fringes; green turned to variations of almost-black, shifted and crouched, clustering in gangs and aggressive formations tensed and primed to jumpiness.

Up ahead a four-legged beast walked impossibly towards her, resolving into a teenage couple hanging on to each other. They posed no threat, K decided, but as she and they walked towards each other, the couple showed no hint or likelihood of stepping aside or even altering their direction slightly. At the last moment, K chose to step aside into the wet grass to avoid collision, angry and humiliated.

However, even in that gross dimness, it struck her that they had not even half-looked at her. She wanted to hurl insults after them. But, had they even noticed her at all? Was that it? The darkness that thickened all around her? Was her shadow-protector with her again? Safer than under the street lights; she was invisible in the gloom!

She saw and acknowledged the shorn trunks and the dank ponds in the murk and bitterness. She was darkness and darkness was her; she was darkness held in darkness's embrace. She was the opposite of all their sharp and bright symmetries, their tyger-tygers burning bright in the new town of the light. She *was* night. Forget your immortal hands and eyes, she was dark and she was untouchable and she was proud.

Safe and invisible now, she was painfully conscious of how the vulnerability of appearance was with her at all other times; now she was shielded, she was more aware than ever of how at risk she always felt, at a low grumbling level most of the time and then spiking into fear, every time she was in public. Aware of just how much those jitters hunted her; because invisible like now, she *knew* no Swan could appear.

K could hear the brook, now the birds were silenced. K could glimpse, every now and again, its grey-green slimy body as it slipped through the cleavage in the plane. It had the look of a muscle cleaned of skin and fat. It was flexing, pulling through the earth channel. It pulled her along with it. It was a hypnosis. Believe in me, shut your eyes and believe in me.

Turn left under the bridge carrying Childs Way and immediately left up the grass bank to Childs Way, turning left along the Redway until just before the Fox Milne roundabout; then follow the Redway downhill and turn right through the underpass marked for Middleton, go straight on past the fire station on your right, take the second road, left, along Noon Layer Drive (walking on the grass verge for a while), turn left down Tanfield Lane, cross the bridge over Tongwell St. and through the local centre. Before the bridge with the large triangular structure, turn left along the footpath (with sign 'Broughton Brook') with Broughton Brook on your right. At a triangular junction take the right-hand path.

It began to rain, suddenly and fiercely. The darkness did not shield her against showers. K sheltered under the bridge and tried to understand what was happening to her. Why she was hiding under a bridge in the dark on the edge of the city. She was tired. Her mind reverted to older ways of thinking. Accountancy took over, creeping up within her: was she 100% darkness or was there a 'mark up'? Was she the bottom line, the net earnings, turnover or rate of profit? Did the darkness have value of use or value of exchange? Could she put a number on transcendence?

Almost as soon as it was falling, the rain stopped.

THEY STILL DON'T UNDERSTAND WHAT THEY HAVE DONE 2 THEMSELVES

RACIST HONKY

A white thing, all legs and cavernous mouth, was crawling out of the concrete under the London Road flyover. It smelled of men's wee. The greasy grey water of the brook ran beside it. K looked at it twice; the second time uncertain if what she thought was a mouth was an eye.

The café was just closing for the night. Behind the counter there was a collage of iconic Italian buildings and objects: a Vespa, the Leaning Tower of Pisa, the Fontana di Trevi where Sylvia cavorts in the pool and anoints Marcello's head with water from the fountain, destroys their dream and triggers the dawn; Marcello returns Sylvia to her fiancé. Ah, *la dolce vita*! The good life – was that what all these passengers thought they might be travelling to?

At the two metal bollards painted yellow take the right fork under the bridge (below City Street, A5130) signposted for Coachway and Brook Furlong. Follow the path under the bridge, with the brook immediately on your right, and follow it further around and over the metal bridge (crossing the brook), following the path straight on to the Coachway building, enter the building perhaps for some refreshment at Café Expresso.

Around fifty to a hundred people were stood; many of them were holding candles. There was some hushed chatter, but mostly there was just silence and the flickering of tiny ticks of flame. Had there been a power cut, K wondered? But the lights around the Coachway building were all still blazing. The small crowd were stood at the far edge of the car park, as if they had been pushed to the limit, unconsciously arranged by the fan of parking bays.

A woman approached K and asked if she wanted a candle.

"What's this about?"

"It's a young man who died in suspicious circumstances."

"What kind of..."

K noted that the crowd was mostly composed of women, with some children. A young girl on a man's shoulders. Some of the women were preparing to launch purple sky lanterns.

"Very sad, very odd really. I mean, be fair, he obviously were no saint..."

"Did you know him?"

"No, I'm a friend of a friend of the family."

"Poor things."

"Yeh. There was some friction, but they loved him. He'd been seeing another woman, no one's perfect, anyway, that'd come to an end, and then he was arrested for making a nuisance of himself. Then he was locked up, no charge. Next day, something like the same thing happens again, he's been drinking and the police are called. There's no charge again, but this time, rather than put him in the cells, what do they do? They drop him off here in the middle of the night, no phone, no cash, that's what we understand... five miles from home... it says in the local paper... strange thing to do. Anyway, two days later the police found him in the stream here, dead. Thing is, like, the family's been asking for the CCTV footage and they keep being told there isn't none; eleven cameras and he doesn't appear."

"Like he disappeared?"

"Like he just doesn't show up. I think there's pictures, but he's not on any of them."

"Is this the young guy I saw in the poster, in the football kit?"

"Yeh, in his kit. Yeh, that'd be him."

"Mixed race guy?"

"I think so. From the photos, looks like it, doesn't it?"

"They just threw him back in the grid, except he didn't have a car to join it..."

"He couldn't have driven a car, dear... And no one thinks much of you if you walk."

"Really?"

"It's been months since it happened, and no one's come forward to say they saw him. Apparently. I reckon if you don't have a car, the people round here reckon you're a nobody, they figure you can't afford the bus to the assessment centre, that sorta attitude. He was good at football. Up Tattenhoe, I think. Good angler, he was a bloke, y'know... his friends say they liked him, and in a second he'd slipped off the radar, gone, that's how quick it can be, tell me how that happens?"

K was pretty sure that if they checked the cctv hard drives now there would only be blankness where she had been.

A lantern took off beside them into the dark night. It burned for a while, climbing and drifting out beyond the motorway and the edge of the city, beyond the outer grid, and then – very abruptly – it went out. At some point it would turn back to paper and wire, falling into a field or a brook, burned and tattered, dropped from the sky.

K did have a credit card. The Coachway was perched at the edge of the city. It would be very easy, Junction 14, M1, to step into the flow to somewhere else, on a far bigger grid.

To her left, K could see down to the grey-green water of the brook, and the path she had walked beneath the bridge; there were these tiny loops in life's journey that could catch you round the ankle and pull you down and down, pull you in, pull you under. All the lights at the junction were at red; their reflection in the wet road sanguine.

The giant freestanding walls were a little like maybe something you prayed at, or those walls that they unloaded fighter jets behind, in case the guns went off accidentally. She felt power just in the shapes; the flattish expanses, impressively dulled by the lights from the road. They felt armed. There was a stringy metal sculpture at the front – as if the statues of the Fontana di Trevi had been scorched and hollowed out by fire, or had cracked and fallen apart over aeons – three human figures were holding up something; maybe it was a horn without cream or perhaps it was a giant car suspension. Above all the traffic noise K heard the word "eee-las-teee-cit-eee" as if it were being stretched out across a long surface of flat water. Around the small lakes, there were herons standing hunched in the darkness, their long beaks on their chests, hunting in their dreams.

Exit the building towards the coach stops under the canopy and turn right across the three sections of pedestrian crossing then left along the pavement as it bends to the right following Coachway Road, to the T-junction with City Street. Cross City Street at the pedestrian crossing, turn right along City Street towards the Northfield roundabout, then left down the Redway parallel with Childs Way. Turn left into the paved pathway (passing a large freestanding wall on your left) along the front of the Regus building, past a sculpture (three figures holding a spiral) on your right. When you reach another large freestanding wall on your right, cut left across the grass and take the wooden walkway over the pond.

Up by the road there was an empty hoarding; its sign had gone, fallen apart or removed, and only its grid remained; it was an apocalyptic map of MK. A vision of a Woughton-like hollow future; just the roads left. On the other side of the H6 a white BMW was stuck like an over-evolved insect on the showroom wall.

K found a blue rucksack at the edge of the path, just within the brambles. She picked it up by the loop at the top, felt its weight, unzipped the main part. On the top was a lunchbox with the remnants of recent sandwiches. K zipped it back up and returned it to the bushes. An inexplicable scattering of boiled potatoes.

There was the Shell garage again, now on the other side of the H6. This was the first time that K had noticed that there was no word "Shell" on the garage at all, just an image of a shell. K did not know that the particular shell, that of the scallop, was the badge of Christian pilgrims, otherwise she might have been more struck by its appropriateness to her own quest and the shrines that seemed all the time to retreat from her. Instead, she tried to think what wordless image of what thing could best represent her psychographic programme.

K had chosen to walk on the grass verge rather than the Redway, which is how she saw the sign for the Holiday Inn Express again and came to fall asleep on one of their beds without the energy to undress. She had lost her protective shadow somewhere around the lakes and was keeping close to the lights. Maybe one of the herons had caught it. Crossing to the hotel sign, standing underneath it and looking up, which K reckoned very few people ever did – like the grid of the empty hoarding, it placed her on a map of stars – it struck K how close she was to the office for her meeting at Fox Milne, how late she was, and how small the margins were in her universe.

At the end of the walkway turn right and walk left along the grass verge, then under a gantry (Max Height 2.0M). At the end of this road turn right up a small grassed obstruction and immediately right down the wooden duckboard and carry on along the pathway. Bear slightly left at the junction of paths, take the underpass signed for 'Northfield', follow the Redway around to the left, signed to 'CMK'.

> Follow the Redway as it bends to the right, then turn left through the underpass signed for 'Fox Milne'. The Redway bends to the left, take the second path on the right (it turns very sharp right and goes through a line of small concrete bollards), follow it under the Holiday Inn Express sign on four white pillars, and carry straight on.

In the night, K dreamed that she was in the comedy movie 'Planes, Trains and Automobiles' with John Candy, who was played by her boss, Tracy Renshaw; when she woke six hours later she thought she had lost most of her sight, before realising that her head was wedged between the wall and four pillows. She struggled to get the creases out of her trousers, before eating a huge fried breakfast. She would walk it off, very slowly, on her way to her afternoon presentation in Wymbush, skirting the lake and down through Pennyland. That way the creases would fall out of her suit.

It was a sunny day. The lines of Land Rovers glistened on what had been wasteground the last time K had driven along this way. From her car, she had not – how could she? – noticed how the trees on the verge outside the giant Coca Cola factory were shaped like the walls of a high-ceiling cathedral nave. In the ferny grass the giant discs of a cable drum were laid out like Ophelia drowned in the brook. The factory shone, as if it had been opened that week. K walked through the gates and towards the reception; a young man walked out to meet her as if heading off trouble. The factory was not new at all; it had been there, he thought, for, maybe, forty-seven years. K laughed at herself, to settle the guard. He seemed to appreciate the gesture and responded with courtesy.

The aroma from the Ball Corporation building reminded her of being a kid and the heady smell of marker pen. If she had had her phone she might have learned that the company did everything from wrapping beverages to launching satellites. As cosmic delivery men, like that lost Amazon man, they might have appreciated the reach of her psychic programme. But she did not have her phone, which made it all the more serendipitous that at the moment she was passing their factory, K was thinking that the image that best represented her programme was a star. Though, she conceded, stars are all versions of the Sun. Maybe the image she was searching for was a circle; or an orange disc. She had not realised until then that smells had shapes.

In the empty showroom on the corner, beside a skewed lamp post hanging above it like a mantis about to have it as prey, there had been a leak; ceiling tiles had been removed to reveal two squares of blue sky in the roof. Where filthy water had hit the ground it had turned the floor into phantom leopard skin. Outside the showroom, K found a platoon of tiny plastic soldiers, their bazookas and rifles crushed in peculiar ways, a broken necklace and a huge pool of fresh catarrh.

K had parked on pavements, but she had never thought, before now, that that might force pedestrians into the road.

Somehow, in the Sun, it felt fine to walk down tree-lined paths today; if they were leading her to an altar, OK, after her sleep she felt ready to have it out with the divine.

The bug-headed Xscape was sat on the horizon; as always.

Pass between the Holiday Inn and World Vision buildings. Turn right along Opal Drive, bearing left at the next junction (keep the ornamental pond to your right) and turn right onto the grass verge beside the V11 (Tongwell St.), crossing the road (carefully!) using the central reservation just to your right and taking the immediate left turn into Northfield Drive. Turn left at the next road junction (also Northfield Drive) and turn left at the next road junction (still Northfield Drive).

At the junction with Tongwell St. turn right along the Redway. Follow it to the left through the underpass signed 'Fox Milne', then to the right, through the underpass signed 'Willen'. Go straight on along the path with a central yellow bollard and black ones to the sides.

At the car park bear right up the slip road to Tongwell St. Turn right along the Redway following it down and around to the right and go straight on at the junction of paths and up so you are walking alongside the Portway (H5) crossing the bridge over the lake and then turning sharp right down the path signed 'Willen Lake – North'.

Take the left path as you approach the water's edge in front of you. Follow the path around to the right, over a small footbridge between the North and South lakes. Take the left-hand path at the next junction of paths. Follow this path, parallel with the shore of the lake (on your left).

DO NOT COME INTO CONTACT WITH ALGAL SCUM

K studied the diagrams describing the operations of the flood control system. Though she could see the elegant shape of the Peace Pagoda on the opposite shore, there was something even more elegant, for her, in the concrete structures of the system. The ramps and curves, walls and weirs, the raising engine and the run-off slope. They were nostalgic and primitive; like the wall at the Regus company building. As if for a functional structure they had drawn on the discarded blueprint for a chapel, a temple or a cursus.

In the event of a flood, the system automatically raised the gate between the river and the lake, then the water poured into the lake over a side weir. But if the lake began to flood, the water would rise over an emergency spillway – where the path was lowered below its usual level around the lake – and then the water would spill back into the river.

There was a swan in the weir; a real feathery one.

Further down the lakeside path towards Willen, on the concrete wall at the beginning of the spillway, were three faded graffiti figures greeting passers-by and preparing them for the possibility of entering the water grid. The first was a one-eyed blue monolith commanding the visitor to…

OPEN YOUR MIND

…the second was a snake with a lingham head set within a horseshoe and the third wore horns, had the serpentine S horseshoe logo – or it might have been a number 5 – at the centre of its chest and carried a trident with EAK! sprayed at the end of its barbs; it might have been Shiva, the destroyer of evil and the transformer of the universe. It might have been anything, really.

K was happy. The intuition of the city that she had received at Jury's Inn was still bright in her mind. It was not a literal map in her head, she realised that now, but a pointer to tendencies; including some very old ones that were still shaping the modern materials. Her meetings – and terrorisation – with and by her various hallucinations were not symptoms of her own anxieties, but were solid things from the city. Animals and sculptures and attitudes that were actually and materially present and active and alive in it, quite different from hopes or dreams. The solid structures of the flood defence system had helped K to realise all this; they were so concrete, and yet the simplicity of their shapes was almost how ideas might be if they were made of concrete. The things K had seen, and fled, and touched were the constituents of the present not of the future. They were hallucinations that were burdens you carried if you wished to see.

K had also learned that the map of light was not necessarily the fastest way to anywhere, and indeed she had yet to arrive anywhere with the help of it; but it was the *best* way, the illuminated and enlightened way. Using the map she would skirt around the lake, bending herself to its reflections, just as light bent in relation to great bodies of mass, feeling the curve through Great Linford, Stantonbury and Bradwell and K would join up with her colleagues for the afternoon meeting in Wymbush. They would already be blaming her, they were always running her down, her colleagues; it would do them good to fend for themselves for a couple of meetings. Then they might appreciate her contribution a little more in future and that would make the whole team stronger. She thought she might make that point to them when they next met.

K was approaching the village of Willen; there was something comforting about these soft tissues of oldness in the machine of the city. The church towers, the village greens, the pub or two with decent food, the pinkish fading of the old-fashioned bricks, the thatched roofs, the alien architectures of the eighteenth-century houses, the occasional convertible to be jealous of. At Willen, though, there was beauty.

K, in a day and a bit, had seen many extraordinary, striking and exciting things. She had experienced the exceptional to be found in the ordinary, been awed and surprised and terrified, but she knew immediately that the church at Willen – dedicated to St Mary Magdalene – was something different, was beautiful. Despite the funny bump at one end, which made K think they might have added an extension for a utility room or a jacuzzi, the church was elegant in all its proportions. The work of a really great fashion designer, but in bricks...

> **Walk straight on through the flood control structure (following the sign to Willen Village), turning left at the next junction of paths, then bearing right at the information board and then turning left onto Milton Road. Up the hill, with the grass area and a small obelisk on the left, turn left into the churchyard of St Mary Magdalene Church, going through the churchyard with the church on your right.**

The moment the thought struck, there was a terrifying cracking and bursting and breaking. The apse which had irked K fell on its face and the rest of the 250,000 bricks – one for each soul in the city of MK – began to float free of its architectural form. First the simple nave and then the ornamented tower parted and moved independently in the background of the blue sky, before they in turn divided into their many constituent parts, hovering and circulating among themselves, and then reassembling in brick form the church's architect, Robert Hooke. His wig in layered curls, his long face and hatchet nose, popping eyes and strained lips, his body slightly crooked. He stood high above K, his triangular head haloed by the Sun. His frock coat, in clay red, hung just above the gravestones.

"Young mistress!"

His voice was hot, dry and dusty.

"It is the great prerogative of Mankind above all other creatures that we are not only able to behold the works of Nature, or barely to sustain our lives by them, but we have also the power of considering, comparing, altering, assisting and improving them to various uses. This peculiar privilege is capable of being refined by Art. That by such artificial Instruments and Methods, we may, in some manner, make reparation for the mischiefs and imperfections of Mankind."

The great Brick-Hooke bent at the waist and leaned his face, like a narrow detached house with a thatch of fired clay, over K's dwarfed frame.

"Am I right in the thought that you, mistress, have such a moral enterprise in mind?"

"You could put it like that!"

"Ah. 'Put it like that' – yes! We 'put' an idea, as we might 'put' a part into an engine, or lay a stone to contribute the meanest of foundations whereupon others may raise far nobler superstructures, or grind a glass that others might see much more than ourselves, or... better still, that most hazardous of Enterprises, raise Axioms and Theories..."

"We will go beyond theories."

"How so?"

Two fists of brickwork clanked against two sides of a waist of fired sand and clay.

"Up until now, theories – of information, of physics, genetics, society – have always returned to their 'mean foundations', as you call them, in matter. What I am presenting to you this morning..."

K gulped. At the realisation that she had slipped into making her pitch and was addressing the First Great Scientist as if he were a board of directors.

"...sir, professor, this is a qualitative leap beyond technology, whether that be of pumps and microscopes or binary codes, mainframes and cooled servers... a leap to pure experience, to art beyond artificiality, to a direct realisation of ideas of matter in emotions themselves, available even to the mischievous, if I may, by the means of an augmented reality with the aim of transcending to a supra-reality. Then we will kick away the ladder, burn our boats, sever our own roots and together, our differences settled, enter virtuality. Professor, we can deliver that to a church, a school, a corporation, a palace or a rented flat through a one-stop terminal."

Brick-Hooke straightened and threw his arms wide.

"I have sought such remedies myself. But, mistress, beware the hazard I speak of now; that in mending the Imperfections of Knowledge your measures prove destructive to Reason and Judgement."

K thrust her hands into the pockets of her jacket.

"Professor, human beings will always fall short in terms of reason and judgement! They are not computers! So, our plan is to remove the imperfection, the human being will play no part in any reasoning; the technology will do all that, and the human – consumer, if you like – will do what they do best, what they were born to do: experience. Pure feeling, unencumbered by knowledge or judgement."

The Architect lifted a chimney-like finger to a wall-like chin.

"Come away with me, mistress, we must to Sandy Napier at Great Linford. Only he can judge if you have found the philosopher's stone or made a design for a public madhouse."

Beckoning with a sweep of masonry, Brick-Hooke turned and began to stride towards the priory, his foundation feet falling either side of the tree lined church path. K ran after him.

> Leave the churchyard through the metal gates (opposite the front door to the church) and walk down the pebble path between the trees, noting the field with a black bench and erratic stone through a metal gate to your left.

"Not so fast! I'm not as big as you!"

"You will be, if what you say is true! You will take your place among the Titans!"

K ran full tilt out through the church gate, following the brick Talos, and down the straight bowered path towards St Michael's Priory, as if tumbling down a luscious rabbit hole of limes and emeralds and jades, stumbling and sprinting in equal parts along the gravel path. Almost at the road, a stone, nearly as tall as K, rolled onto the path and stopped her dead in her tracks. It tumbled forwards and spoke.

"Stop, stop... or maybe pause... pause would be fine, really... or go on if you need to... I only wanted to say... stop... or think about it anyway... listen to me going on... after all, what place would I have in your plan? I mean, maybe my appearance, or the concept of 'erratic', I suppose that might be part of it... jolly good luck to you, really! But look at me! Touch me! Go on!"

The stone leaned forward. K extended a nervous fingertip. The stone was cold beneath her touch.

"Not from round here, you see! Came down with the glaciers... you can feel my smoothness, my rough edges torn from me by other rough edges..."

K felt very cold. The shadow of Brick-Hooke had fallen upon her, though the roof of leaves above was so rich she could only feel his presence by its blotting out of the Sun.

The erratic seemed to settle a little into the gravel.

"Under your plan, dear soul," said the erratic, "you would of course feel my smoothness – I suppose that's something, but it's also nothing – because I would not be there; that may not mean a lot to you, or anyone else, but it means a lot to me! Speaking as a thing. Not that anyone takes any notice of stones, but they should! Geologists love us! Kids throw us into the sea on beaches... think what you would be losing... fish don't care! It might not seem much... nothing at all really in the great scheme of things... who knows..."

K sidestepped the capricious stone, which attempted to swivel in the gravel and fell on what K had been assuming was its face. She joined Brick-Hooke, glancing guiltily back at the erratic, which was beginning to roll back to its place beside an arty black bench in a half-hidden field. As she turned away, Brick-Hooke was bemoaning the loss of the church library in a fire, but K was distracted by a poster on a lamp post: "There's no such thing as the Dog Poo Fairy!" it screamed, with a visual edict to owners to pick up their pets' ordure: if you don't do something yourself, no one else is going to do it for you. Duly noted, thought K.

"... words are powerful, but fire is more so, words cannot eat fire, but fire can eat words..."

On their progress to Great Linford, a striking duo who scared the horses in a private paddock, Hooke advised K to patent her ideas and secure recognition for them, complaining bitterly how he had done all the heavy lifting on Gravity for Isaac Newton but "the end-is-nigh moonstruck fool!" had stolen all the credit. "Name recognition – crucial to your legacy, mistress!"

Brick-Hooke spoke of the grid he had devised for the rebuilding of London after the Great Fire of 1666, striding over playing fields and the local centre, tip-toeing carefully along the towpath and stepping over the H3.

"Some fellows conceived the conflagration as a cleansing by fire, a cleaning out of the stables, a chance for the spiritualising of space. Sir Christopher – Wren that is, St Paul's you know – if allowed, might have realised such an ideal in bricks and stone. Exigencies and pragmatics were set in our path. Only in this city have our ideals, though not our taste – have you seen some of the offices? – been realised in parts. Perhaps you have understood, as we did not, that it is not the opportunity of idealism that comes by cleansing fire, but rather that fire – or Sun in proximity – *is* its realisation! Come, look."

He beckoned K across the humped back bridge and to her left. There were two small buildings, almost as beautiful and apparently mercurial as St Mary Magdalene. Brick kilns in a subdued sunny orange. K noticed how the ground around the kilns had the manicured look of mown lawns round medieval ruins: surreal and formal. She found it hard to concentrate on Hooke's disquisition on the extreme temperatures of upward of 1000 degrees centigrade, the chemical transformations of clay and sand in such heat, the swelling of the iron brace around the superstructure of the kiln and the long days of cooling after. At each point he raised eyebrows like lintels, as if there were some special quality to the industrial process, before turning up Willen Lane with K tagging along behind him.

Where the path meets Newport Rd. turn right down Newport Rd. and left into and along Linford Lane, which becomes a footpath. Follow this footpath, with sports fields on your left. At the end, cross over Beaufort Drive and Granville Square and through the covered arch with the Ship Ashore pub on your right. Carry on through the two underpasses (beneath Brickhill St. and Dansteed Way) and straight on (with a slight dogleg to right and left) up Bec Lane (on the pavement on the left-hand side of the road). Cross over St Stephen's Drive – this path (in a straight line) continues for about 200 metres until you see the canal ahead of you.

Join the canal towpath turning right immediately under the footbridge. Follow the towpath (water on your left) under another footbridge and under the roadbridge carrying Monks Way (H3), then turn left over the canal at the next footbridge, and turn left down the footpath to the George Price brick kilns.

Retrace your steps from the brick kilns and turn left down Willen Lane (there is no name sign) between a small car park on your right and a white house on your left. After about 300 metres, where three footpaths and a private access road to a field cross the lane, turn right onto the footpath and immediately left, following the footpath through the underpass beneath Marsh Drive. Carry straight on past a pond on the left until you get to the sign on your left showing that this is Harpers Lane.

At this sign, bear right onto a path that is the start of Great Linford High Street, initially with The Green on your immediate left, at the end of The Green bearing right along the High Street. After you pass The Nag's Head on your left, go through the white gate immediately ahead of you, and go straight on along the footpath with Linford Manor on your right. At the next junction of paths take the path to your left and walk up the incline to pass between the two yellowish stone gate houses and then turn immediately right and walk towards the gap between the almshouses on the right and the churchyard of St Andrews on the left.

Passing through the underpass beneath Marsh Drive, K was relieved to be out of the company of such a weighty intellectual architecture for a few moments. Once on the other side Bricke-Hooke continued to lecture K on the need to attend carefully to what his friend Napier would say.

"He died the year before I was born; you might say he handed the torch to me. Be wary, mistress, his is an *earlier* kind of thinking than mine; try not to judge him by the assumptions of your own time. Do not be too inflexible, and not too flexible. When I was flexible they stole my ideas, when I was inflexible they claimed I was the thief! Learn from the metal spring; if you pull it just enough it remains serviceable, if you pull it too hard you destroy its special quality – its eelasticitee – you burst the cells within it, those tiny enclosures in which its qualities live and pray constantly – do not bring the whole body of the material monastery down upon your head..."

"Robert!"

K looked about. She had been distracted by the village – another old anomaly! Whole other villages were buried beneath this one! Beyond, the park, the manor and gatehouses, a small figure stood between the line of almshouses and the churchyard wall. The quarter of a million bricks of Robert Hooke's design, one for each city soul, were once more suspended, gently revolving in a dance around each other, only then to tumble across the sky backwards towards Willen, combining in a simple box and an elegant tower. K followed their rambling disappearance and then turned back to the source of the gentle voice, thinking at first it might have come from one of three tall figures, their wooden heads topped with an obelisk and rusty metal blades, standing in the garden of an almshouse.

"C..c..come in..."

But it was Sandy Napier, the sixteenth-century vicar, his hands bandaged, a leather apron strapped over his vestments. He led K gently through the South Door of St Andrew's church. Inside, the church was a laboratory; huge glasses, tubes, flutes and sieves were suspended on giant callipers or hung in nets. Steam moved about in gangs and slow gunges dripped from strangled pipettes. On the tiled floor lay huge piles of putrefaction; while on great panes of opaque glass thick concoctions bubbled and fermented. Napier blushed, tugged nervously at his long beard, and then pulled gloves over his bloodied hands and swiped away a gobbet of acid eating through his apron.

"Purges, amulets, occasional blood-lettings... er... have been most efficacious in the treatment of noble lunatics, but what if a universal elixir were placed, through prayer, into all our hands? I see you are confused. I am not a good preacher, better that I show you what I mean..."

He pumped an organ with his blistered foot, his hairy toes manipulating the bellows, and a fierce tongue of flame leapt from a small furnace causing all the tubes to spit and foam. Napier recoiled, avoiding a tiny ball of the fiery totality which chased his head and zinged about the nave in a looping journey not unlike K's own.

"It's not a map of light I'm following", she thought. "It's a map of fire; there is danger as well as destinations in it."

With smouldering hair, Napier dashed back into the fray. Somewhere between sublimation and exaltation, the experiment hung in the balance.

Within the thicket of the green fugs that crowded about the seven rows of tubes and their attendant flasks, all throbbing and bubbling, a figure appeared, hanging in the miasma, distinguished by the turquoise of its eyes and the whiteness of its wings, mouthing words to K, handing powders and other materials to Napier. K could not read its lips, but the unreal angel smiled upon her apologetically as if to say "not now, but later".

Into a bowl Napier tossed fur and eggs and began to beat the mixture; from the mess tiny creatures, like miniature terrapins with horses' heads, flew on wings of soft ectoplasmic meringue. Napier plucked them from the air, flung them into the furnace, at which they burst into white doves.

"Almost... almost there," said the alchemist.

He caught the seven doves in his gloves and placed them, one by one, in a cage of sugar-glass, sprinkling them, through the bars, with iron filings which fell from them without adhesion.

"Pure," yelled Napier, "without attraction! One last ingredient."

He turned to K expectantly. K was aware that this was not reality. She had left reality outside with the three wooden fetishes in the almshouse garden, their rusty and inefficient wire operations agitated in a rising late morning wind. She had left reality with the WILD FLOWER AREA in the graveyard, and the headstone carved with an octopus sun crawling over a quarried text:

BLESSED ARE THE PURE IN HEART FOR THEY
SHALL SEE GOD.

As the Sun got higher in the sky the air had become disturbed.

K stared back at Napier. "The moment has passed", declared the alchemist. "It is time to put away the equipment until another time." He unplugged the bellows, threw down his gloves, cut through the strap of his apron with a knife, drained golden fluid into a bucket and tipped it into a drain in the floor of the church.

"You may go."

The wooden door in the South Wall blew open and, after a moment of uncertain disappointment, K walked out into the blustery sunlight. The trees were tall, the grass bright green, the demonic-looking angel above the porch stared down on K without patience or forgiveness. The lesson was clear; seize your chance, *carpe diem*, timing is everything.

> **Passing the three wooden sculptures on your right, take the path between the churchyard wall of St Andrews and the end of the almshouses.**

K looked for somewhere to sit or hide. She needed to have time to herself; the hallucinations had been crowding in all morning. For a while she leaned upon the iron railing around a Universal Bench Mark, just beyond the church wall, approximately secular. There was something consoling about the Ordnance Survey's pre-Einsteinian faith in a universe that might be fixed: "HEIGHT ABOVE DATUM". Then, confronted by a rough monument of stones in loops on the path ahead, she climbed up to another, smaller stone circle, on a low mound, and then followed its rough path down the other side and into the void of the old quarry there. For a minute or so K was pleased to share being a symptom of someone else's great work; and now, she thought to herself, it was time to get on with her own.

As if in joy, the six bells of St Andrews rang out.

Suggested end point of Walk 3: St Andrews
Church, Great Linford.

Walk 4

Suggested start point: St Andrews Church, Great Linford.

Estimated walking time: 3 hours.

K joined the track of the old railway, its metal rails and wooden sleepers long gone; raised above the neighbouring back gardens on one side and a brief woodland floor on the other. She missed the arcane design and Utopian Alphabet,

IS 'TIME TO ESCAPE' MEANT TO FIRE OUR COMING AGE?

on the National Cycle Path Network milepost, with Mercury ascendant to Venus floating in a cosmic eye exploding light like a failing star; these were symbols from Sandy Napier's sixteenth century and the fixed orbits and motionless Sun from the Copernican system, measured by solar deities like Nergal and Shamash, the son of Sin, and still in circulation.

K, instead, dwelled on the chaos of individual and family lives measured out in piles of broken furniture and general trash dropped over back fences, and piled up in back gardens and alleyways. She struggled to imagine the effects of living among ruined things; even in the office she could not see a ring of coffee around a mug without wiping it up.

K sat by the ponds thinking about coffee and furniture. She thought about her flat, and how her world had expanded very quickly; she was sitting on a rock not a sofa, watching ripples like spreading coffee rings, not a box set on Netflix.

The thought of coffee rings interrupted her reverie; there was a figure in black skirting the water's opposite edge and there were swans. K made her way swiftly up the side of the field towards the cemetery.

Beyond the churchyard, take the path to the left, past the OS benchmark 15 metres beyond the churchyard wall, set behind railings on the left of the path. Just before you come to a large arrangement of stones, climb up to 'Ruthie's bench' on the left of the path, a bench surrounded by stones, then either follow a muddy path down into the trees and bear right through the old quarry, or come down from 'Ruthie's bench' the way you went up, turn immediately left along the path you were taking and then immediately left again and follow the mud path through the trees; in both cases bearing around to the right, and back to the main path, with a small stone circle immediately to your right.

Take a left turn along the path running parallel to the canal until you reach the former railway bridge, then bear left up onto the pathway that crosses the old bridge (Railway Walk), but turn left along it and away from the bridge, passing the red signpost for the National Cycle Network, going in the direction of New Bradwell. After about 300 metres, opposite the underpass signed for 'Stantonbury' on the left, take a right turn at the end of the hedge and go through the gap in the fence to the ponds in Stonepit Field. Sit on the stones there a while.

K was impressed by the Shinto grave, with offerings of rice and oranges, by a black and white plastic bollard and yet another fake stone circle with a massive O2 mast in the centre. Who knew? Local phone users were communicating via the grave. Near the giant lych gate, a sculptor, perhaps forewarned of the height of the plinth, had carved the head of a World War I soldier – far from the dwarfed spectator below – out of proportion with the rest of its body. While the intention had, presumably, been to even up the visual effect, the calculations were misjudged and the infantryman looked like the plaything of his generals, a giant doll, the human equivalent of a nodding dog on a dashboard.

Walking down the verge, K was shocked, again, by the proximity of hurtling metal. At the junction, she realised she must have driven over this point many times and never had any sense that she was passing over a track that ran for miles through the dermis of the city, a 'rat run' for walkers. Dropping down to the path, K quickly left the traffic noise behind, the Walk stretching ahead to a vanishing point, and immersing in a green birth tunnel of birdsong. On one side she passed an armchair thrown into bulrushes and was overtaken by narrowboats: at the tiller of the first a couple were having a row while their two children cavorted on the bow; on the second another two children, glowing in lifejackets, were restrained in the arms of a grandmother, fearful of losing them to the future. Childhood, thought K, is a time to escape and fire our coming adulthood.

In the distance something like a pair of thick snakes advanced along the walk towards her. As they got nearer, K could see what they were: a pair of legs, dressed in old moleskin trousers and heavy leather boots. Trousers and footwear were caked with local soil which fell away as the legs strode blindly on. K asked the legs where they were going. They said they belonged to a train driver called Samuel

Kendall, but had become separated from the greater part of their owner in an accident with a steam locomotive on the tracks near Castlethorpe, in the cemetery of which village they had been buried. Unforgivably, the rest of Kendall, on his death, had been buried at Wolverton and the legs, cheated of a reunion in the grave, had pulled themselves out by their own boot straps and set off in search of the rest of themselves. K was sympathetic but explained that they were walking in the wrong direction. The legs, undeterred, turned and headed off the way they had come. K watched as they strode out of sight.

Walk away from the ponds, staying within the fields. Go in the same direction as before, but parallel with Railway Walk (a hedge between you and the path) until you reach the far left corner of the furthest field. Take the small path with a metal railing, leading into the cemetery. Walk through the graves, past the O2 mast and on to the WWI monument with a stone soldier. Turn right through the covered gate and left along Wolverton Rd. Cross Saxon St. (V7), very briefly follow Newport Rd. before turning left down the footpath and then right along Railway Walk again. When the canal appears on your right, turn right, then go left to follow the canalside path. Turn back onto Railway Walk when you see the next gap to it on your left, continuing rightwards in your original direction. Turn sharp left up the path to houses with steep roofs and flat frontages.

"Still looking good, eh?"

"I'm sorry?"

"The houses – their shaping, massing, their visual impact, quite emotional and surprising even now... some problems with materials, after all these years, to be expected, but the basic impact is still... striking? What do you think?"

"Well, when you put it like that..."

K looked again at the vaguely triangular shape, its top sliced off and knocked on its side; she remembered the concrete shape on the path to All Saints church at Milton Keynes Village.

"'Put it', yes, when I 'put' the idea to you, it places it somehow, localises it, gives it an identity. That was the plan! What do you do?"

"Me?"

He looked around, puzzled, then back to K.

"Yes, you..."

He turned to the young child, perhaps a granddaughter, who was stood between the handles of his wheelchair, and mugged a look of exasperation.

"I was a planner here," he continued, "a trained architect – these are mine! Are you walking in the city? If you can ignore the horrendous Barratt Homes clones, there are still plenty of things to see: the houses that look like numbers, Tinkers Bridge – I like the simplicity of the single-pitched roofs, the rhythm of the trees and the pillars in the centre – Marshworth is a little haven, Netherfield was a bit too stark but, hey, what did we know? We were building on a ratio of only five to an acre, the green spaces we allowed then!! Of the new stuff, Oxley Woods isn't bad. But much of the rest is a betrayal of the master plan. They've started filling in the underpasses, for God's sake! And what about our tallest tree rule?"

"What was that?"

"That the tallest building in the city should not exceed the height of its tallest tree. Not much attention to that, you say, but when they first tried to break it at the Jury's Inn site, the scaffold around the building came crashing down like a bomb had gone off; don't tell me the trees were not angry... same as when they built across Midsummer Boulevard, that was never intended, the Sun should have a clear run..."

The elderly man swept a few locks of greyish-brown hair across his forehead and straightened a polka-dot collar. His papery hands brushed crumbs from the lapels of his jacket.

"Have you seen the flat roofs at Marshworth? The H shapes there?"

"No..."

"You should! What did you say you did?"

"I didn't, but I'm also a kind of architect. I design software for product and service delivery..."

"Interesting!"

The tiny girl placed her hand on the old man's shoulder and he placed his hand, reassuringly, over hers.

"All that was once done mechanically; roads, vehicles, depots," he mused, "very energy inefficient... will any of that be left by the time you are my age?"

"Will anyone be left by then?"

He laughed; squeezed the hand of the child a little tighter.

"When I began the sketch for these homes, everyone at the time thought we'd be flying around using jetpacks; turned out that would only be James Bond and Michael Jackson. How can you be sure your work won't turn out like that?"

"Good question."

K checked the wedge of houses.

"Do people enjoy living in them?"

The architect shrugged.

"Everyone is different."

K thought again.

"I think your problem was symmetry. People are... well, you just said it... different, not symmetrical, or only very approximately so, two arms, two legs, one on each side, so we add inconstancy to the software, betrayal even, we add a ghost here and there. Our programmes do not dictate, they cannot be dictated to, they don't plan and they are not plannable..."

"You said you were a programmer..."

"That's different from design, programming is noughts and ones, there's no reality, no imagined trapezoid, just notions, impulses to sound out, surveying everything, incorporating the whims and peculiarities of the markets. Maths. Unlike designs, our programmes are as perverse as people. Why would anyone throw broken furniture into their back garden? There's no excuse. Exactly! There is no 'why' to people; trying to force people into a why is how, occasionally, you end up building concentration camps, or, more often, inhospitable housing estates."

"Our estates are not inhospitable. People love to live here!"

"You said everyone was different..."

"How can you be so confident of *your* ideas?" He looked to the child for reassurance. "You'll learn..."

"Because... to be frank? ...we stole them off the people we are selling them to. They will love our ideas, they will seem to them like long lost friends."

"Clever, but you are wrong. Our problem was never symmetry, nor messing with what at the time were fashionable ideas about sun worship, Stonehenge and so on; our problem was inconsistency. You think you can build a brave new world that way, that's the way we just ruined one here."

As if responding to a signal, the child released the brake of the wheelchair and swung her grandfather around, setting off back up the path – the old man open-mouthed with surprise.

K shouted after them.

"Who shall I say if they ask me who I met?"

The wheelchair paused. The old man twisted in his seat.

"The Great Architect!"

He pulled up one of the legs of his trousers and poked out his tongue. A moment later they were gone.

Walk past the front of the terrace of the houses with sharply sloping roofs and turn right after the garages without walls on your right, past the 'Wylie Drop In' on your right, up Kingsfold, past Pepper Hill School on your right, and turn right down Ashwood (with giant trees in the gardens to the right) and then right at the T-junction, briefly along Bradwell Road before turning almost immediately left (opposite Wylie End) into the drive (Mill Lane) to the grounds of the New Bradwell Cricket Club. Passing derelict tennis courts on your left and skirting around the right-hand edge of the club buildings, follow the edge of the sports field. Take the gap in the hedge to the right onto a small path and turn right to the windmill.

K had seen the sails of the windmill above the trees that flanked the changing rooms and pavilion. Then she had all but forgotten about them; taken by the squidgy abjection of the derelict tennis court, its tarmac and tramlines lost in moss, a dumping ground for failed fast food stalls. So, when she dipped through the hedge on the edge of the sports field, the sight of the vast stone building, its four sails motionless and poised, had hit her like a symmetrical punch dead between the eyes. She saw stars; or to be more precise, she saw a star with many points. The windmill was a triangle with its top knocked off, the sails a radiating Sun sat like a cosmic eye on top. Driven by the invisible.

K was reading from the information board how by 1876 the windmill was unprofitable and its moment had passed, when she sensed a presence. A wingless Gabriel was stood beside her, reading the board.

"The last gasp of an old industry," he said.

"They kept it, why would they do that? In 1876?"

"It doesn't say. Perhaps they were nostalgic, but I doubt it. I imagine knocking it down was more trouble than it was worth."

K looked at Gabriel. She recognised his face from the smoke in the church, but she had not taken in how handsome he was. Even wingless, he had an air of superhuman beauty, as if he had been found fossilised in amber, broken from the golden age. His bronze face glowed under the blue sky. Inside, silently, K was laughing cruelly at herself. She did not usually like tall men.

"Are you interested in the Industrial Revolution?" she asked, for something to say.

"Not particularly", he apologised, "perhaps in general." His voice rang like the tenor bell at St Andrews. "I'm here for the annual general meeting of the Vintage Lawnmower Club..."

"Don't mess with me!"

"Why shouldn't I be?"

"What kind of people are members of a club for... what? ...vintage lawnmowers!"

"People like me!"

"There are no people like you!"

"You have a point..."

And he effortlessly floated from the information board to the plinth around the windmill once used to reach and repair the sails, bearing K up with him, holding her hand. She had not noticed him take her hand, and when they landed she did not notice him release it.

"Quite a view from here!"

K looked out to the spiky church tower at Wolverton, radio masts like rakes on the sky and a tall thin white tower. She looked down again and they were hovering above the sails of the windmill.

"I can't hang around," she complained. "I have to get to Wymbush for an afternoon meeting."

"What a pity," he said, as they landed back on the sloping green incline to the windmill. "I'm going in the opposite direction. We are meeting at Willen Park, for a mow."

"I don't believe you for one minute!"

The angel laughed and the windmill's sails began to turn.

"Well, it was nice to meet you, if only briefly."

"The pleasure was entirely mine."

Impetuously, K kissed the angel's cheek. His wings unfolded, as wide and tall as the sails, their feathers stiffened by a rising breeze.

"I recognised you from the church..."

Gabriel folded his wings, but his arms continued to hold her.

"The Reverend Napier is not my master; when he calls, I come, not in order to serve him, but to save him. He thinks he will escape his mortal coil to a heavenly radiance, but he is in danger of burning his soul. Those of us who have known such children of light, such morning stars, believing they would rather serve in imaginary heavens than reign in their bodies... they rob us of our temples. There are no lawnmowers in paradise, K. Would you begrudge me my lawnmowers?"

"I wouldn't begrudge you anything..."

And for a moment, it seemed to K that she and Gabriel were hovering above Willen Park while below them a thousand gardeners in oily overalls performed curling snake-like turns in an exquisite labyrinthine choreography of modest machines.

"What will y..."

There was no one there. She was alone, stood before the windmill, its sails as still as before. A blackbird sang somewhere. The wind had dropped. Freshly cut grass beneath her feet eased to take her weight. She felt her mortality; that she might have stretched her springs too far. That there was no snapping back this time. She sauntered down the green, with the smell of grass in her nostrils, the vista opening up just as she had imagined it from above the windmill – church, masts and tower – but there was no Gabriel to transport her. She never walked anywhere! Her legs were so stiff and tired now, her feet were sore, and her clothes in dire need of changing. She pulled herself up from her ennui, stiffened her back and threw her best foot forwards into the green.

Leave the windmill, walking back along the small path down the incline, cross Nightingale Crescent and take the footbridge (signposted to Stony Stratford) over Grafton Street (with the canal in an aqueduct running parallel and to the right). You are now back on the Railway Walk. Follow it straight on at the end of the bridge, with the canal a little way off and on your right, parallel to the path.

She had not realised that one of the bridges above Grafton Street carried boats over the heads of drivers! The weirdness of that! Like a swimming pool in a cloud!

Opposite a path on your left to houses, with an (empty) information board, take a right-hand turn onto an informal mud-path and turn left along the bank of the canal, (possibly passing a small tepee and discarded Christmas tree on your left), with a view to a large block of flats up ahead. Where the canal-side dirt path joins a main path on your left, turn sharply left and just before a junction of paths, take a very small dirt path (climbing over the stile/fence) through the trees to your right; climb over fallen boughs across the path and take the steps made of logs to your right, up to a small clearing with a mound.

The car sounds, once again, faded quickly. The walk beside the water revived K's spirits. Bees worked the airwaves. She glided down a tunnel of bramble. She was absurdly moved by a miniature tepee made of three sticks and foliage at the side of the path, dwarfed by a huge block of flats in the distance. This vista seemed to mean something, but K had no idea what it was. Narrowboats were gliding smoothly by on her right; one called 'UKANDO: The Forgotten Realms'. 'UKANDO'? 'You can do'? The Sun shone. A few thin white clouds haloed the tower block. She was accompanied for a while by a bright yellow butterfly in jumbled flight. She heard, but could not see, a multitude of birds.

She stopped dead, rigid with fear.

A train roared like fury. Across the metalled path that ran alongside her muddy one and rejoined the canal with its battleship grey water, some way ahead, just before it passed under the concrete bridge that carried the four lines of railway track, was the Swan. His chest puffed up, His neck arched, His wings hung out. He let out a scream of triumph, lowered His beak and began to run towards K.

She turned onto the metalled path and began to run back towards the Railway Walk she wished now she had never left. She looked about her frantically as she sprinted, for someone to help her, for some chapel or fortress or maze that might afford her sanctuary, but there was nothing and no one. She thought of trying to leap from the canal bank onto one of the...

Somehow He had got ahead of her. She was approaching the tarmac triangle where her path met the Railway Walk, but He had already got there. His granite wings spread wide, angrily snorting, honking and hissing. K turned back, but there was nothing but path behind her, no cover of any kind, there was the track down to the tiny tepee, precious little use that was, and to the other side a kind of informal stile, a broken fence, onto the roughest of paths through a low cover of branches. K took it, hurdling the fence and crashing along the notional path, leaping over fallen boughs, and bounding frantically up a rough set of earth and log steps covered in lime green moss and orange fungi.

At the top there was a small clearing, with a patch of burned ground marked out by three sticks, though it looked as though there had been more, and there were trails of hazard tape along the ground; it might have been a crime scene. There was a small mound in the centre of the clearing and K ran behind it, though it afforded her very little protection. She wished she had picked up one of the large sticks. She looked about her; the only things on the ground were square carpet tiles and small rectangular shapes of corrugated iron, both of which had had numbers sprayed on them. She could see 6, 7, 12, 9, 8, 11...

The beak and then the neck of the stone Swan, His granite chain swinging, appeared over the top step of the log staircase. K felt the blinding vacuum of the unknown growing all around her. She was falling into the unthinkable light and she had no idea how to help herself. Trampling through the barricade tape, the Swan seemed to grow more human-like, a blank and hairless head and chest thrusting up from His back and rising above His rigid neck, until the whole horror stood some seven feet or more tall at the pate of its featureless skull.

It shook itself.

"See Me! Ἰδὲ! How can your vague fingers push This feathered glory from your trembling flesh?"

In desperation K grabbed one of the carpet tiles and flung it at the Swan. From where she had removed it a small lizard ran out, then another, and then another, until a crowd of them were issuing from the grass, forming a surging shining silvery green carpet that advanced upon the Swan. The swarm of lizards grew quickly to tens and then to hundreds, surging all around the sculpted bird which tried in vain to sweep them away with His wings.

"My loins engender the broken wall, the burning tower! Ο Αγαμέμνονας είναι νεκρός!" hissed the Swan, as little reptiles surged up His chest and nipped at the feathers in His neck. Still, He stomped forward on hard palmate feet, crushing lizards here and there, advancing at K. She seized up a corrugated iron 13 from the side of the small mound and drew it back.

From a hole exposed by the lifting of the iron sheet a large rat, a foot long from nose to tip of tail, ran out, followed by another. Just like the lizards the rats swarmed quickly and raced in concert at the Swan. For whatever reason, the rats made a far greater impression on the Swan than the lizards, and He was thrown into a desperate retreat, racing down the slope of the mound, attempting to gain flight, crashing through the branches of a tree, barely vaulting a dilapidated cast iron fence close to the metalled path, before stumbling on the green and skidaddling over the surface of the canal, rats falling from His plumage, just missing the bows of a narrowboat and, with feet peddling frantically, He escaped into the air with a frightened honk.

"Βοήθεια!"

K turned, absurdly, to thank the rats and lizards. For a moment they seemed to have taken up two approximate forms; the lizards into a triceratops, the rats into one huge rat, two metres tall and wearing evening dress. K blinked. The figures dissolved into squirming masses of rodents and reptiles which proceeded to fall over each other in their efforts to get back to their holes and under their tiles. In a moment K was alone, wondering where she was and why.

The numbers, the tape, the mound full of holes; it was some kind of survey. The shape of the land felt vaguely prehistoric, there was even a small cairn of stones overgrown with moss and nettles. What did she care what it was?

> **Walk down the log steps and turn left back to the main path, then right along the main path and right at the triangle-junction of paths (back onto Railway Walk). Go through a pillared entrance to the estate (Blue Bridge), through the houses, cross Culbertson Lane, and through the underpass beneath Miller's Way (with a view to the railway on your right). Follow the path past Lullingstone Drive on your left, across Constantine Way into Loughton Valley Park with the reconstructed outline (low walls) of Bancroft Roman Villa on your left.**

Hardly wanting to double back and meet the Swan again, she tried to continue on the rough path at the bottom of the log steps, but it quickly brought her to an impossibly tangled thicket with tight thin trunks and watery green light, the rotted and rusted cadaver of a motorbike snapping at her ankles. Reluctantly, she turned around and found her way back to the Railway Walk which, to her relief, quickly led her, through a roofed and pillared gate, into suburbia, primroses growing in the grime on a less used patch of Redway. She, like them, would survive a hostile world.

K imagined a Mausoleum up on the hill. Commanding the skyline the way that Xscape had for her the day before. This time she was in the hilltop structure looking down and not looked down upon. She imagined the relief of shedding a vulnerable and imperfect body and becoming a blameless, blemished, untouchable witness. She was by the information board in the pseudo-ruins of Bancroft Roman Villa, imagining her presence up on the hill and far in the past; around her were two-foot high rockery walls marking excavated foundations. They adeptly gave to a space of off-putting significance the tidy, cosy feel of a garden centre. But there was something decidedly not fresh...

K was physically shaken by a gut-inverting stench. A nightmare parody of Gabriel creeping up behind her at the Bradwell Windmill. She warily looked around and there, stood directly behind her, was a tiny woman with a pixie haircut dressed in what had been a white tutu and purple ballet slippers, covered from head to foot in excrement.

"Mother of pearl! What the hell happened to you?"

"Nothing. I'm the Dog Poo Fairy! You know, they say there's no such thing as me? Well, here I am!"

"I can smell you!"

"What did you expect? Rose water?"

"No just... nothing... I expected no smell..."

"You think your perfect mausoleum on the hill would have been sanitised? You think the pretty picture on the board there is how it would have been? That they put the bodies on the hill so the dead could keep a watch over their loved ones below? Or to blow away their smell of rotting flesh? If you live on Planet Antiseptic, your broccoli individually wrapped in plastic, plastered from head to foot with Paco Rabanne 1 Million Stick and intimate deodorant..."

"I have never..."

"Never seen a dead body outside of a cinema screen? Never seen your evening meal slaughtered... I could go on."

She waved a sinister looking small plastic sack to emphasise her point.

"Leave me alone... why can't you all leave me alone?"

K turned and ran down the crazy paving path, huge tears dropping from her eyelids.

"We never will! As long as you need us!"

> Carry straight on down to and across a wooden walkway over the river (a small weir to the left), then take the steps/path to the right and then follow the path signed for 'Loughton Valley Park South' following the route of the river (with the river on your right). Just before the underpass there is a view to the Concrete Cows in a field to your right across the river. Go through the underpass signed 'Bradwell', then take the right turn signed 'Bradwell Abbey', across the bridge over the river, and under the stone railway bridge (passing an electricity pylon and substations to your right).

Outside the gate of the electricity substation, K stood and listened to the comforting hum of stray magnetic fields resonating in the casings of the transformers; she dried her eyes and focused on her breathing. Inhaling in short bursts, her hand to her mouth inhibited her gulps, until she once again felt calm.

How had everything gone this wrong?

She was so very close to the industrial estate at Wymbush. She could still see the afterburn of the map of fire that she had glimpsed outside Jury's Inn; she knew exactly where she was on it. She could tell from the position of the Sun in the sky that she was not late; she had plenty of time. But the interruptions and attacks upon her had intensified; from physical assault to emotional temptation by way of mystical bamboozlement. They were really trying to get inside every part of her.

She wanted to pray to the angel, but she knew that that would be fatal. If he came, she was lost to him. If he did not – and how could he when he did not exist? – she would feel distraught and weakened before the meeting at Wymbush. Why were her hallucinations so confusing? The chemist in the church telling her to disappear into fire, the angel giving her good reason to have a body and a soul, the Dog Poo Fairy wanting her to think about dead bodies. And what were the legs about? No, she would not pray, she would be strong in herself and confident in the programme that she had helped to create – that, be frank, she was the Great Architect of! – and she would power her way to Wymbush and sell that programme like no programme had ever been sold before.

She would re-charge herself!

K placed a hand on the porcelain core of a support insulator; it was lying in the dust beside the spiked gates of the substation, as if it had been tossed over the fence or placed for loading and promptly forgotten, abandoned like a piece of fly-tipped furniture. The enamel on the china discs was chipped, but the object still had some power in it; a jewel of the high wires. K placed her other hand onto its warm porcelain surface and felt a surge of self-confidence racing along her wires, running between her substations and lighting up her map. She gazed up at the giant pylon, standing like a Titan, but what impressed her was the sign on the metal fence:

CAUTION

THIS SITE HAS BEEN IDENTIFIED AS

COMPLEX.

K could not help but notice a similarity between the architecture of the substation and that of the Roman Mausoleum.

Turn left at the sign to 'The Abbey', go through the wooden gate, crossing Swan's(!) Way Bridleway, and carry straight on until you see the chapel (under repair) on your left. Walk over to it.

~#~

Suggested end point for Walk 4: Bradwell Abbey, Alston Drive.

Walk 5

Suggested start point: Bradwell Abbey, Alston Drive

Estimated walking time: 2½ hours

The white tarpaulin, hung around the roof of the chapel on a cuboid plank and scaffold structure, looked very weird to K. Not only was it torn, exposing the metal poles and wooden planks holding it in place, but its material had perished in the Sun. It looked like the skin on a blow-torched surface. If there was once a serious conservation project here – she knew from the information board at Bancroft that material from the Roman Mausoleum might have been used in the building – it must have been forgotten. Which seemed strange for something like an Abbey, K thought. That kind of name generally attracted serious money, serious institutions. This looked like budget shortfall or bankruptcy or some massive change of priorities. This was the kind of place that needed her programme!

K was surprised to find that the chapel was accessible at all; around on the far side of the tiny stone building a guide was holding aside a flapping plastic sheet and ushering a small group of visitors through the scaffold-cluttered entrance. K neatly attached herself to the end of the queue. Inside, the building seemed taller than it was long. It drew the eye upwards to the paintings on its walls. The guide began to describe them, but she broke off to explain how the images had been recovered. The chapel, the only part of the sacred buildings of the Abbey still standing, had been in use as a storage shed by a local farmer. He had stored sacks of fertiliser there, and when rain broke through the roof it had fallen on a sack of chemicals; this had released a corrosive gas that attacked the lime wash Puritans had plastered over the 'idolatrous' images and they began to reappear.

A chemical rather than an alchemical miracle.

K looked up to the roof and there were cherubs and seraphs blowing trumpets in heaven and there was Gabriel, his hands and facial features as mild as truth.

"The medieval folk who came here", explained the guide, wheezily, and pointing vaguely towards Two Mile Ash, "on pilgrimage, diverting off Watling Street to get a blessing, would stand and listen to the services at the niche over there. It was enough that they should see someone who could see someone who could see the elevation of the host, such was the magic of the bread! Only the monks were allowed inside the church itself. If those simple souls had seen these images emerging from behind the walls, what a shock they would have had! They certainly would not have understood chemical processes – even the most educated among them did not understand that gold's glistening was not the activity of the metal itself – they would have believed that the images had their own life. Perhaps the priests and wealthier, more educated folk would have understood, or remembered, that the images here had been created by human hands and not by angels, but even they might not have been privy to the secrets of the artists and architects, masons and illustrators who made them; even they might have thought there was something unworldly about the images themselves and about the manner of their making. But it was plain old fertiliser and the very human skills of depiction and deception... the images are not, themselves, alive..."

As if to spite her, figures began to peel away from the walls, the pilgrims and St Anne stepping down to the tiles of the chapel. High up, the flimsy figure of St Michael weighed insubstantial souls in a jelly-like set of scales. The descent of various figures revealed a giant M and six flowers which in turn floated free, the M marching erratically about the chapel like the legs of Samuel Kendall.

The flowers formed around the head of a saint teaching a tiny Virgin Mary; the saint formed shapes with her fingers and Mary repeated the gestures. The guide then turned to the painting of the Annunciation and a mature Mary floated down, followed by the Archangel Gabriel, who winked at K, a dove suspended in the air between the two. While all the other figures were like films of jelly, Gabriel looked fleshy and real, he shook the long red curls of his head, his elegant features smiled and his arms and fingers pointed delicately about the chapel.

"It varies how much you see, dependent on the weather", explained the guide.

"Where are Gabriel's wings?" asked a visitor, and Gabriel lit up, sheets of flame erupting from between his shoulder blades and leaping up the sides of the chapel, the heat illuminating the entire wall of clouds, trumpets and crowds of pilgrims marching, throwing down their staffs and kneeling, holding up wax effigies of heads, legs and arms.

"Shut the front door!" thought K to herself. "On the... altar thing, by the canal, that must have been a votive offering!"

The whole city within a city had a whole other city inside of it; how did that fit in with K's plan? She was pitching against the hidden world!

She began to crab carefully down the side of the chapel, but before she could get near the door the guide was herding the visitors outside. Again K tried to inveigle herself onto the end of the procession, but the guide motioned her to stay behind. No sooner had the last of the visitors exited than a procession of monks entered, all hooded, an odd collection of lumpy giants and less than child-sized clerics, one was trailing a leathery tail from beneath its habit and another, similarly, exhibited clawed and hairy feet. If their hoods revealed anything, it was faces in deep shadow, except for one whose face *was* only shadow. As these figures solemnly marched in they brought with them a smell of zoos.

Once assembled, they disrobed and revealed themselves: the two-metre tall rat in a suit, the Dog Poo Fairy, Bill the Triceratops, Gabriel, the two legs of Samuel Kendall, the erratic rock and the shadow sporting a pair of black goggles. The wheezing woman guide was their spokesperson.

"K!"

"You know who I am?"

"Who you are is your own business. We know *what* you are doing!" The guide put her hand to her chest to control her breathing. "And we are your protectors..."

K looked up and down the line of motley superheroes; the spectral paintings from the walls hung about them like rippling energy.

"From that Swan?"

"Bad myths!" interjected the Dog Poo Fairy.

"Bad art!" echoed Bill with a roar.

"Yes, K, from the Swan..." the guide confirmed.

"But we are... well, mostly... protecting you from yourself..." continued the glacial stone.

"What?"

"And from the stress of delivering the programme..."

"What the erratic is trying to say," the guide interpreted, "is that we want to avoid you becoming a victim of your own programme."

K had not considered that as a possibility before.

"And is Robert Hooke and the alchemist, and the planner... are they part of your... group?"

"No, my dear," the guide explained, "they are *your* allies, not ours."

"There is a war in heaven!"

Gabriel's voice, in the confines of the chapel, fell on K like warm chocolate.

"They see in your programme the opportunity to pursue their formalism and we see the potential to enhance the material world. You will eventually have to choose between the two paths; the one into fire and the other into..."

Gabriel paused.

"Slime, goo, afterbirth and slobber, bodily juices!" The Dog Poo Fairy completed the angel's sentence.

"Box sets, champagne, Michelangelo's 'David' and sweet chilli crisps." Gabriel re-completed it.

"Which is why, my dear, we put ourselves at your service. Without your consent, I'm afraid, and we apologise, but there was no time, and you would not have understood. We watched you pass the Jerk & Grill at Eaglestone; would you have stood and listened to us then? In the state you were in? No. But knowing what you do now, experiencing what you have, and the more stable state you're in – I'm right, aren't I? – you... you... excuse me..."

The guide reached into her handbag, retrieved an asthma inhaler and puffed it into her mouth, inhaled deeply and recovered herself.

"...you are ready. To join us. Be part of us, one of us."

"Go on!" urged the Dog Poo Fairy, unappealingly.

"We cannot win in heaven," implored Gabriel brightly, "unless we have angels on earth."

"Help us blow a couple of raspberries at the planners!" roared the Triceratops and shook its horns, so vigorously that the shadow had to dodge their swinging tips.

"I'll let you know. I'll seriously consider your offer, I really will, I promise, but I need a little time. This has all come as a shock, I am sure you can understand that, but I will, I assure you, properly consider your amazing offer... Thank you, thank you, thank you..."

K feared that the chapel door would be locked, but it opened easily and, mostly in relief, but with some disappointment at her faintheartedness, she pushed back the plastic sheeting and ran across the grass, slipping on the pebbles that now marked the absent Abbey's outline, and escaped between the remaining priory buildings and the old barn, past some metal squid things and walked swiftly over the footbridge towards the industrial estate.

The names of the companies – I AM WATER, DECO EXPRESS, CITY COMFORT and the logo – six hexagons around a single hexagon – for a firm selling pistons and pulleys and motion control systems all seemed oppressively significant to K. As if they were there to symbolically disapprove of her running away from an invitation to join the... whatever they were... The roar and swoosh of four lanes of traffic, exciting and meaningless, like action movies – everything moves, little changes – left her feeling comfortingly numb. On Garamonde Drive, between giant industrial units with grumbling and fretting ventilation ducts, she was hailed. It was the last group of people she wanted to see right now; the team of reps of which she was a member. They came running across to her, accelerating as they got closer, as if they were anxious she might try to run away.

"Where have you been?"

"Are you OK?"

"What happened to you?"

"They found your car abandoned outside Jury's..."

"Was it because we didn't wait for you?"

Things had not been going well. K could tell from their faces. None of them would admit to any figures, but they were clearly anxious to have her back; they thought that she was going to save the day for them. What the hell did *they* know? She had just been asked to join an alliance of superheroes! Materialists Assemble, something like that, although their membership criteria were rather liberal. She was tempted to tell them "I'm the only superhero here, you guys need to hero up!" but she doubted they would understand; they had never appreciated her for what she was, for the things she brought to them from the richness of her heritage and background and by the sharpness of her survival instincts. No, they were just anxious that their not waiting had screwed it up for the company!

"You think I can save you?" she told them. They seemed to take a collective step backwards.

"Are you OK..."

"I can't save you. Unless you are prepared to be honest with yourselves. There's a war in heaven – which side are you on? Have you chosen or do you think you can stay neutral? There can be no freeloaders on the programme, you understand that, right? No one is going to buy from anyone who has not recognised the programme as their personal salvation. If they can't see it working for you, how can they see it working for them? What is coming is something entirely new, a leap of faith made by executives who lack knowledge of the future. The programme is no respecter of persons or their drive or their energy or their purchasing power. This is a revolution; the introduction of an economy of authenticity and directness, an economy of passion... if you people are not in touch with your own feelings, if you are not prepared to be at the mercy of your own impulses here, right here in the street, in the meeting room, in the bedroom, then you will not be able to sell this product... because there is no product there! We are selling desire, and we are selling satisfaction, and we are selling the disappearance of any gap between the two, so, in future, time will not be measured in days to delivery or minutes in a queue or even seconds to upload or buffer, but in humanly imperceptible nano-seconds... the augmented body will be *directly* plugged into the industry of sensations and subtle sensibilities... that is why you must never hesitate! What I am realising, and this is essential fieldwork I am conducting out there, is that the augmented body will also be plugged directly into the city... I had rather assumed, like alchemists or Jesus freaks and meditation types, that the body would simply fall away and transcend itself by moving into pure feeling, but now I realise that thingness will return... not as a transport system or an architecture, but as... I'm not sure what as... that's why I must get back to my research... just give me a day or two and I'll sort it out..."

"What?"

"We don't have a day or two, we have appointments all this week..."

"Postpone them or you'll pitch the programme wrong..."

"Why is it always you that has the integrity, K?"

"I don't know, Giles... I don't think I am especially chosen... I think it must be that the rest of you are just not self-aware enough."

And with that she turned on her heels and began to walk off down the Redway, the loud grumbles beginning to fade away behind her, just as though she were leaving behind the traffic noise of an obsolete era, an archaic stage in evolution. None of them tried to call her back, until she heard a new voice. Her boss's.

"K!!!!!!!!"

Tracy Renshaw was stood at the wing of her convertible, door swung open, engine running. A slight breeze played at the curved lapels and cuffs of her immaculate Hugo Boss 'Jabina' jacket, her pixie blonde haircut unmoved by a gentle zephyr.

"What the hell has got into you?"

K knew that she should run back to her, but she also knew that the energy of retreat would surrender everything to Ms Renshaw. K would be sucked back into the team. There was a war in heaven, but the sides on earth were only just being drawn up. Things weren't clear enough there yet.

"I can't right now, Tracy..."

"Get back in there, the execs are waiting for your presentation!"

"I'll let you know. I'll seriously consider your offer, I really will, I promise, but I need a little time. This has all come as a shock, the significance, the implication of the programme, the need to balance the psychic effects of the programme and the social and material consequences... you need to walk, Tracy, to see what the possibilities of things are... we are going to destroy all that, but we don't have to, the programme can raise the customer to the level of angels, I've seen the possibilities! Thank you, thank you..."

"Stop, K, stop! Listen to yourself!"

Renshaw took her hand off the bonnet and straightened.

"I don't know what you've seen or what's happened to you, but I would like you come back to the office and talk with us about it. Maybe, you have found... K, wait! Listen to me. Maybe you have found something we haven't thought of, we can always improve the programme by pooling our ideas and working as a team..."

The gaggle of reps tightened to Renshaw, they looked to K a little like the superheroes and she wondered if she saw a horn and a flash of malicious Sun.

"Give me a day or two, please!"

"We don't have a day or two! We can talk later, but we have a pitch to make right now! People are waiting! Angels? Psychics? A war in heaven? A *war in heaven*! K, we are going to help them sell *bathrooms*!"

K ran from their vulgarity.

Racing out onto the Redway, the vehicle noise was less than it should have been. Cars shot by but something, maybe the yellow blossom on the shrubs or the green of the verges, dazzled their engines. K was worried that she was exposed on the long path and hid in a clump of fir trees near the underpasses, listening to seven types of birdcall. She watched as a line of four alloy-wheeled, rescued wrecks with big-bore exhausts growled up to the roundabout, then raced off towards Stanton Wood. A fifth struggled after them, its boy racer peering, bewildered and frustrated, under the sunstrip; arriving too late at the roundabout it circled five times, then shot off, its Cosworth body kit flashing in the high Sun, misguidedly, towards Crownhill.

K was turned away at the Kam Tong Garden restaurant; the kitchen had just closed. She had settled on the idea of eating a slow meal – it came to her watching people throwing handfuls of indigestible processed bread, like a white infection, onto the surface of Lodge Lake – while she considered her options. There were meetings next day; in an office in the centre in the morning, then another out at Willen Lake later. If she could reorganise her presentation, then she could get the clients to see that they were selling sensations, rituals of cleansing, deep pleasure, body transitioning, immersion, theatre, reintegration in aqueous ecology. Not just bathrooms. What happened in their bathrooms tomorrow would happen in boardrooms, workplaces, cinemas and bedrooms – everywhere! – the day after. K knew that the programme had started out as a more efficient way of moving bathrooms, connecting the right bathers to the right baths, but how could no one else see that it was becoming something much, much bigger?

Instead of reorganising over a slow, sweet and sticky meal, she felt hungry and disorganised. Straining up the incline of Attingham Hill, for the first time a feeling of homogenous suburban ennui settled over her, dispelled immediately by the sight of a structure at the top of the climb that was slowly coming into focus.

From the chapel, walk behind and through the City Discovery Centre buildings and out along their main drive, turning left along Alston Drive, then right at the sign to 'Wymbush', crossing Alston Drive and up the raised footpath straight ahead, over the footbridge over Monks Way. Follow the footpath across Garamonde Drive, along the Redway signed to 'Two Mile Ash'.

Just before the next underpass turn left along the Redway parallel with Great Monks St. As you approach the underpass to your right (just before Lodge Roundabout) turn left and follow the path, bending to the right, through the underpass signed for 'Great Holm'. Then follow the path (the Circular Walk, to your right as you emerge from the underpass) around the edge of Lodge Lake, keeping the lake on your left. Pass Lakeview Village Green and Kam Tong Garden restaurant, both on your right. Follow the restaurant around to the right and walk up Attingham Hill (ignoring turnings off) until the brick obelisk comes into view. Walk to the obelisk.

An enigmatic red brick, thirty-foot tall obelisk – representing 'a frozen ray of sunlight' she discovered online at the hotel, later – was spattered with white extrusions, as if a giant seagull was habitually perched on the top. Something in the rain was reacting with the lime in the mortar between the bricks and tiny white stalactites had formed on its ridges. As she approached the summit of the hill and the base of the unnamed and unexplained monument, an ornament for no one and nothing in particular, K began to recognise some of the members of a teenage gang who were shooing away a pair of female dowsers complaining about negative energies and the inappropriateness of an obelisk on a modern estate.

Among those sending the two packing down Highgrove Hill, waving their rods in frustration – "you look out, it's not the obelisk doing it, the negative energies are *feeding* the obelisk, it's doing a good job neutralising them!!" – were Robert Brick-Hooke (who looked as if he were a distant relation of the obelisk's), the Reverend Sandy Napier, the planner in the wheelchair with his child-carer, absence and blankness from the Coachway, the boy racer that K had seen just a little earlier, before the lake, lost at Lodge Roundabout, a Wall-E-like drone and a figure she had not seen before: a pixellated Buddhist monk.

"It's sending all the negative energies up into the ether!"

The women disappeared out of sight.

"What are you doing here?"

"We could ask the same question of you, mistress!" Napier gazed intently at her.

"What my eminent and studious friend is trying to say," the figure of Brick-Hooke ground out, "is that our great desire is that you, mistress, avoid becoming a victim of your own programme."

K had heard of and considered that possibility already, and was frightened by it.

"What about the Tyrannosaurus and the Archangel Gabriel..."

"Triceratops", Robert Hooke corrected.

"Whatever. And the giant rat! Won't they protect me?"

"No, my dear," the blankness explained, "they are protecting their own agenda, we are your allies. We want you to fulfil your programme. They don't."

"Yes, but both of you seem to think I may become a victim of it!"

"There is a war in heaven." Sandy Napier's voice, in the blustery exposure of Attingham Hill, was thinner and more papery than ever. She wanted to fall on his arguments and tear them into pieces. "Your so-called protectors see in your programme a threat to their own materialistic self-interests and the continuation of their secular, consumerist and spiritually corrupted carnality."

The boy racer looked nervous and turned to the blankness for reassurance.

"What's the matter with pleasure?" K asked.

"It isn't knowledge," explained the planner, earnestly, leaning forward in his wheelchair.

"It's a kind of knowledge..." K retorted.

The child placed her hand on the planner's arm and eased him back.

Napier continued: "Your so-called protectors see this as an opportunity to increase the power of the material world in their possession; they are interested only in profits and selling bathrooms. What we understand, mistress, is that your programme has the potential to transcend such things..."

"It has beauty, it shapes the world!" declaimed the planner, gesturing to the obelisk.

"It transforms information into form and sensation," Brick-Hooke added, gruffly. The drone blinked enthusiastically. The blankness seemed to encompass the entire obelisk in fervour. The tiny mathematical fragments of priestliness were passionately assembling and reassembling themselves, but into nothing sufficiently coherent to respond except by further permutations.

"What about you?" K asked the boy racer.

"Speed," he said, simply and pointedly, darting nervous glances at the renaissance scholars. "A to B, modifications, lowering."

"You will eventually, very soon probably, have to choose between the two paths; the one into the mire of compromise and commercialism, the other into..."

"Fire?" K interrupted the planner.

"No," replied Napier. "Knowing, pure knowing and..."

He paused.

"Acceleration, coolness, crapping yourself!" The boy racer completed the alchemist's sentence.

"Knowing God, astral travel, communion with the planets, the best tickets to the music of the spheres, the shedding of flesh, ambrosia, visions of eternity", Napier re-completed it.

"Which is why, mistress", continued Brick-Hooke, placing his baked fingers lightly around the shaft of the obelisk, "we put ourselves at the service of your programme, without your licence... A thousand humble apologies! But there is no limit to the compass of your idea, it transcends flesh and commercial contracts, it breaks all laws. Including..." and here he squeezed too tightly and the ben ben stone at the apex of the obelisk threatened to topple off, "those of physics!!"

The obelisk made a crunching sound and tiny white flakes of lime showered down on the allies.

"Join us. Be part of us, one of us."

"It's sick, innit!" urged the boy racer.

"We cannot restore heaven," the alchemist implored, squeakily, "unless we have soldiers of the mind."

The parts of the priest formed the shape of a broken sword, the drone flashed with a dazzling and unnatural brightness.

"Help us blow the system out of the water!" roared the planner, pointing to the sky. "Avebury, Stonehenge, Midsummer Sun! What will you design!"

"I'll let you know," said K, quietly, backing towards Kensington Drive, edging to the side of the road with tree cover. "I'll seriously consider your offer, I really will, I promise, but I need a little time. This is all very new to me. I am sure you can understand that I will have to radically change the business plan, the master plan, the marketing philosophy and strategy will have to be... transcended, but I will, I assure you, properly consider your amazing offer... Thank you, thank you, thank you..."

And she, like the two dowsers, disappeared over the brow of the hill of Great Holm, once out of sight turning into Macintyre Coffee Shop to buy a sandwich and a much-needed take-out flat white; an inoculation against the scrambling of her brains.

Turn left down Kensington Drive, bearing left at the MacIntyre Coffee Shop, then go down Kensington Drive, through the underpass (immediately to the left) signed for 'Loughton' and then turn left down Paynes Drive, and left down Bradwell Road. Finally, turn right down the footpath that runs alongside Loughton Baptist Church.

The door of the chapel was open and from behind the closed door to the service room, came the strains of 'Thine Is The Glory': "Angels in bright raiment rolled the stone away, kept the folded grave-clothes where Thy body lay". K sniffed at her jacket. Through the open door she could see formica-top trestle tables laden with sandwiches and funeral meats and covered with linen, while a regiment of Woods Ware Beryl green cups and saucers stood in parade ground order. If the coffee and sandwich from MacIntyre's had not been quite so good K might have been tempted to help herself; instead, with three separate gangs in pursuit of her – the reps, the allies and the superheroes – she cut down the side of the Baptist chapel into the alley.

> **At the end of the footpath, turn left along Snaith Crescent (no pavement), left down Whitworth Lane and then turn right along Bradwell Rd. Pass a large thatched cottage on the left, then look for the public footpath up a driveway to the right (signed with green 'Public Footpath' posts set back from the road). Follow this, taking the footpath bearing to the left with a tall wooden fence on one side, up to All Saints Church.**

In the shade of a cottage, in the golden hour of Sunlight, a professional photographer was manipulating a young couple; under K's programme no one would ever surrender their image. She tried the church door, it had a lucky horseshoe nailed around the handle; third attempt, third locked church. No one would ever be excluded from the spiritual comfort of *her* programme.

"Hey! Babe!"

K had not recognised him. Her photographer. The one she was dating.

"Excuse me," he told the couple. "Just for two minutes. Take a break."

The couple dropped back into preening infatuation.

"You left me!"

"Babe! I thought I should let you sleep! You were pretty cranky the night before. Where've you been? Are you OK?"

"No, not really."

"O, babe, how?"

"World falling apart. Personal crisis of confidence. Probably going to be sacked. Feel like I'm going insane. War in heaven."

"War in heaven? What's that?"

"Something in my head I need to sort out. And it's really... screwing with my work. Pardon my Dutch."

"French..."

"I just walked out of a company meeting!"

"Babe! You can't do that sort of thing!"

"I know. I should go back and apologise. But I can't. I have to shut up these voices in my head, first. And I've started to see them, too..."

"See what?"

"An angel, a dinosaur, there's a rat too..."

"Can you see them now?"

K looked around the churchyard.

"No."

"That's good, then."

"But I know they're near."

"Look, I've got to work. Can I come over tonight and cook for you? You can have a bath, relax, get back to normal?"

"I'm not sure where I'll be tonight. Maybe not even on this planet. Look, you must get back to your clients. Me too."

"Text me. Wherever you are, I'll come and get you."

"I lost my phone."

"You don't have your phone!!!"

"I know. But it's letting me work things out in my own way. Without anyone telling me how to think. It's giving me space to be..."

"Cranky."

"Yeh." K laughed. "What am I going to do?"

"I don't know what to say."

"Go and make your photographs."

"When you get your phone back, text me, right?"

"Yes."

"Promise?"

"Yes."

"I'm going to be there for you, babe. Just to talk. Cook you dinner. Whatever it takes."

"You're a good man. Your clients are waiting."

The couple had worn out the core of their fascination without a recorder; they brightened as K's lover turned back to them. K felt, abruptly, bereft.

"Amir?"

She turned him around and planted a kiss on his lips and he responded gently, but she felt no better. As she let him sink back into the shadow of the cottage, it was as if he were slipping, drowning, in the dark depths of a lake, as if the Sun were pushing him under and she would never get him back.

"I have to save heaven from the Sun!" she shouted.

The couple began to shift uneasily. Amir checked their nervousness and looked back at K as if to say "don't spoil this for me", she thought. Even her attentive lover would betray her when the sides faced off for the war about heaven. Discovering the old villages hidden inside the city had been such a thrill and surprise when K's adventure began, but now they were starting to disturb her; their weird histories, the vicar of one parish shooting the vicar of another with a bow and penny arrow... how did she know that? At times it was like she was parroting someone else's research. She had not got it off her phone... Was this the type of crap that people would remember about her? That she scared her lover's clients in a churchyard. That she helped sell a lot of bathrooms? That she fought on the wrong side in heaven?

The couple were smiling. Amir made the irritating 'phone me' sign and touched his chest. K mouthed "I will".

Go through the churchyard and turn right down School Lane and immediately go left through a metal gate into the extra graveyard, and through this graveyard to an exit through a metal gate on your left onto Pitcher Lane. Turn left along Pitcher Lane and take the path, to the right, opposite the top of School Lane that runs through two black bollards and past Becket House Nursing Home on your right, along Turvill End. At the T-junction turn right along Linceslade Grove. At the end of the road, cross Redland Drive and bear left up the footpath which bends to the right; turn left over the bridge over the A5 and the railway lines and into Station Square.

The blue sky had been parcelled into thousands of cubes. A flash of red cape in the last brick-orange rays of the Sun; the light was fussing around the fringes of the buildings. K looked around the square and inside the station lobby for places to stay the night, but she knew this was not something that could be done spontaneously; there was a political economy of homelessness here, one in which she had little capital, at least not of the kind that she was willing to invest.

K checked in to Jury's. She had gone so far and got nowhere, she had returned to her starting place as someone else. She still had her credit card. The company had a discount at the Hotel, but she feared to use it in case it was monitored and they came for her. She risked using the laundry service and reception sent a maid to collect her suit and shirt from her room. K washed her underclothes in the bath and dried them over a radiator; she washed down the bath, filled it and lowered herself into the warmth. That was all she needed to know about alchemy.

During the night, as K slept in a bed of troubled sheets, the Sun came out of hiding. It crept around the central grid, patrolling Its zone. There was almost no one around; a cleaner here and there bent over a machine, soundless behind glass, a homeless woman restless on top of a third layer of mattresses, like a princess in a fairy tale disturbed by the tiny fact of her pain. Other than that, the Sun saw only plans, forms, shapes and PCs in sleep mode, the grid in meaningless dreams. These were Its territories, ironically; in the day the optic array was too complicated. At night the Sun could enjoy Its sovereignty over the Earth. It was not a crown that sat easily; for the Sun knew It was dying. It observed the sufferings of the humans exposed by the night – cold, lonely, betrayed and deranged – but these were short. Nasty, brutish sometimes, but always short. The Sun would be dying for aeons. The Sun could not sleep, could not dream, could only burn.

> **Suggested end point of Walk 5: Station Square, Milton Keynes Central railway station.**

Walk 6

Suggested start point: Station Square, Milton Keynes Central railway station

Estimated walking time: 1½ hours

Walk a short way along the side of Station Square, turn right through the 'tunnel' in the building, signed for 'Leisure Plaza', then left along the back of the building and left along its far end, turning right across Elder Gate, skirting to the left of the former Bus Station. Turn right along its back, cut across to the far right corner of the car park, through a gap in the hedge, and bear slightly left through the underpass towards the Jaipur Restaurant.

Turn left along the front of the restaurant and then immediately right onto the mud and grass behind the restaurant, past a bench and around a pond. Pass a black and white dovecote on your left, then turn left and then right on the paths, following a steeply climbing path through ponds and water channels.

Skirt a circular pond, bearing right at the top of the green space to the back of the Avebury Building. Crossing Lower Fourth St., turn right and then left, walking parallel with Avebury Blvd., alongside Witan Gate House, then bear left across the car park and over Witan Gate and through the gap between Zizzi and Loch Fyne Seafood into The Hub. Bear left across the Hub, through the fountains, and exit the hub between Jury's Inn and Travelodge.

K scoffed a sprint breakfast of grapefruit juice, egg and toast and checked out, noting that the cigarette butt had moved to a new square on the blue and darkness chequerboard outside. She still had no idea what it meant, only that all things had a meaning and when you ignored them that became a part of it. It felt good to be striding out in crisp clothes. She had got away with it; she was filled with joy and adrenalin. The hotel had not fallen down, as she feared it might, given the tallest tree rule, and no one had found her there; the two mounted police officers patrolling in Midsummer Boulevard completely ignored her. It was the ironed suit.

She was tempted to revisit the void spaces at the end of Cresswell Lane, but she feared being sucked into an endless loop of the city, and ploughed on up the Boulevard. All night she had dreamed in excruciating detail about her presentation; it went off perfectly and all the execs present were delighted, Renshaw was chastened and ecstatic, contracts were signed on the spot without lawyers and all the time K had been suspicious that the rooms were constructed of thin scaffolded facades on the point of falling down, that the bodies of the execs were shells, and that she was selling a dream within a dream within a dream.

Abruptly vulnerable to gazes, she cut inside the Midsummer Walk building.

There was a film being shot on the walkway above Bannatyne's Health Club. Or, rather, a film about a film. An artist was reconstructing, on a zero budget, scenes that had been filmed here for 'Superman IV: The Quest for Peace' in which Milton Keynes Central railway station had stood in for the United Nations building in New York. On the walkway they were reconstructing a scene from the movie in which the villain Lex Luthor and his nephew

Lenny steal a strand of Superman's super strong hair from a vitrine. It made no sense. If the hair was super strong how could Luthor cut through it with a pair of pliers? Lies and re-creations of useless and meaningless lies.

Under the gaze of the artist's camera, the two avatars for Gene Hackman and Jon Cryer were skulking among the exotic shrubs in the Club's atrium; further back into the shadows of the greenery, just about visible at the edges of the giant palm leaves and tropical fronds, were members of the two gangs of Superheroes and Allies.

The director checked a scene from the 'original' 1987 movie on a monitor, held up the camera and shouted: "I hold the camera up and everything looks the same!"

There was a strong smell of bleach or chlorination rising through the humid air; a chemical purification of the residue of exercising bodies. K had stumbled on a chemical conspiracy in the sweaty heart of MK for the transcendence of physical reality. A conspiracy for the evaporation of material space and the ending of the uniqueness of place by the siphoning off of the citizens' own physical energy! The Superheroes were right, but they were powerless; like Superman, their hair wasn't really very strong! – they were all like Samson and already blind to what was really going on! – only K knew, only K could see, and the only thing the Superheroes would ever be able to do about any of it was to tear down the city around them! To enforce the rule of the tallest tree! And who did that help? The Allies! There was no way out! They were all the enemies of the real, and they were all out to get K and her city MK! She fled.

Sprinting from the triangulations of mystic symbols, public art and earth energies, K almost collided with a woman coming out of the Church of Christ the Cornerstone.

"Entschuldigen!"

Ignoring the woman, K walked very carefully, very normally and very introvertedly, reflecting the least possible amount of light that she could. Even so, the moment she entered Centre:MK, she knew that she must get out of the place very quickly; before they picked her up by pattern recognition programmes or the sixth sense of the guards.

Trying to get out, she found herself caught in dead ends and architectural prostheses. She had taken another wrong turn, not escaping but falling more deeply in. Under the wave roof she felt seasick, and stumbled, brushing the shoulder of a zombie passer-by who failed to notice her. Exiting into Midsummer Boulevard she could not recognise where she was. Where was the orange disk of concrete on which she would perch to text before her meetings in the coffee shops?

The Sun was already high, mad and strong. She ran back into the INTU building and turned right, but the Midsummer Oak and the concrete cows were gone. There was just an empty space there; a crowd milled around the edges, grazing. The city was being undone all around her. She turned and escaped the building by the opposite entrance; passing the cadaver of The Point, the city's skeletal version of Lenin's Mausoleum, every bit as ideal as the architecture of the Roman Mausoleum at the Bancroft site.

The Point was going to be torn down. Freaking hell, they were pulling the whole place down around her; maybe it was all a plan by the Superheroes and she had stupidly, for a moment, thought they were OK.

Turn right up Midsummer Blvd, then right into Midsummer Walk (inside the building) after Zen Garden. Turn left through the building, then right into Bannatyne's, past Bistro and the mural on a pillar. Just before the glass doors with 'bistro live' backwards on them, turn left and go out through the glass doors. Bear left across the square, across the formal garden and two sun symbols in the ground, to the far left corner. Pass the Holiday Inn on your right, exit into the square of the Central Business Exchange, pass the twin sculpture by Eilis O'Connell, 'the space between', up the steps on the far side and through the porte-cochère crossing Midsummer Blvd (under the purple 'Sarsen Stone' on top of one of them, if it is still there). Turn right beside the Job Centre, then left, walking parallel with Saxon Gate to the Church of Christ the Cornerstone.

Turn left, enter the church by the front door, make a circle of the cloister, then exit by the front door. Turn left, walk parallel with Saxon Gate and at Connells (on your left) bear right, take the underpass and bear right past 'The Conversation' by Nicolas Moreton, and into Centre:MK.

Turn left along the arcade, right at Hobbs (on your left) and through the glass doors, momentarily outside, then walk under the wave-like roof of the INTU building, with a view to The Point on your left. Turn to the doors on your right, go outside briefly to the circular flower bed that, at the time of writing, covers an orange concrete disc in the road, then turn around and re-enter INTU, turning right to briefly enter Midsummer Place (site of the Midsummer Oak). Turn around and back into the main lobby area and turn right to exit INTU (with The Point and a view to Xscape on your right). Walk up the pavement parallel with Midsummer Blvd, past 'A Mighty Blow for Freedom' by Michael Sandle.

The part of the open market under Secklow Gate was a bit too much like a zero-budget redux of 'Bladerunner'; K had got into the sequel, but this was not it. The neon strips reflected in the glassy eyes of shoppers. Cutting back through Centre:MK, the circle of silent hanging chimes was horrifying, like looking at the soundlessness of the dead moon. K slowed and walked warily under its copperish armatures; long enough to notice that nobody was noticing, that the people around her were sealed into their own worlds and that everything around had died to them. The Sun was evil, and the city was dedicated to it.

K had been right. The end *had* come. The ground was razed and scorched; where there had been a grove of trees, surrounded by greenery – she remembered it vividly from parking her car repeatedly beside it – there was now only a levelled and ruined patch. It looked like a recently deserted battlefield, not the lush druidic grove that she recalled. Was this a model for the future of the forest inside the city; an end to the resorts of rats and the homeless? She had also noticed along the Railway Walk the signs of a thrashing machine which had been smashing back the 'excess' growth on each side; there was no cover here from the surveillance of Allies and Superheroes.

As she stood in horror at the thrashing down of the trees, she became aware that the morbidity she had felt amongst the shoppers and lookers inside Centre:MK was not a figment of her imagination, or something 'off' about the living residents. Instead it was a visitation by real corpses. The one hundred Saxon bodies buried together in the All Saints churchyard on Willen Road had reassembled and they had now arrived, completing a shambling trek across Woolstone, Springfield and Fishermead. Assembling around the mound, they stood silently; whatever the nature of the justice they had once handed out and the democracy they had enjoyed here at the moot so many hundreds of years ago, that was now as lost as air, words never recorded, expressions on faces that had long rotted, almost no artefacts found. The mound was reticent, nothing of significance had been found that could be used to date the site any more accurately than sometime between the fourth and thirteenth centuries.

The ranks of the Saxon dead stood in silence, unforthcoming, except for the slow peel of their brittle features.

In the pitted faces of the Saxons, K recognised the features of boyfriends and brief lovers, friends and family, people she had taught herself to avoid, ignore or neutralise; memories, sweet and sour, that she had drained. The ranks stood, fragile husks, parodies of seeds.

There was no authenticity to be had from the past. That had always been clear to K. Likewise, the collective plan of the city was compromised; there was no place for her programme in that. She could depend neither on her supporters nor her enemies; and she was unsure how to know which from which.

There was only one truth – and that was the truth of her programme, the subjective life of the individual, that's what the programme was about, releasing the sensual, loving, longing, ambitious, aspiring, hopeful individual into the greatest possibilities of their own desires, not by the simple act of satisfaction – commodities could do that, bathrooms could do that – but by plugging individuals, via virtuality and augmentation, into the ever-expanding potential of their own desires and their own imaginations. The ever-expanding self. A universe in every person. That was why running away was not an act of cowardice, but an expedition to the very farthest boundary of what was yet known by K about K.

Go through the Open Market, turning left at Diwan Mobiles and into the Centre:MK building. Turn left along the arcade, passing under the giant 'Circle of Light' sculpture by Liliane Lijn, then turn right down Crown Walk. At Fraser Hart, turn left down Silbury Arcade passing the large outdoor space on your left, then turn right at Hobbs (shop on your right) and exit Centre:MK and cross Silbury Blvd. under the porte-cochère to the Central Library.

Turn right past 'The Whisper' sculpture by Andre Wallace and then turn left down North 9th St., climbing up the concrete steps on your left and bear right across the waste ground to Secklow Mound, turning right along North Row.

At the end of the buildings on your right, turn right down Lloyds Court, past the 'Black Horse' sculpture by Elisabeth Frink, and bearing slightly left and under the flyover (Silbury Blvd.) enter Centre:MK at Deer Walk, visiting the golden-decorated toilets area straight ahead – with a reconstruction of the Bancroft Roman floor mosaic on the left-hand wall and a cuboid pattern on the floor.

Just before she cut into the corridor with all the palm trees, K thought she saw George Romero, the director of the Living Dead movies, in the big empty exhibition space, chatting with a priest in a dog collar about shopping malls, but that was not possible, because George Romero was dead.

K knew that she was no longer running from, but running to. She was not sure how that was going to work out. She still wanted to do the programme, launch the programme, be part of something bigger, but how could that work out without the programme turning on her? She could not see a way to realising herself in the programme without her disappearing into its digital fire. She ran quickly through the two puzzles, the compass in the privet and the Rose, dodging its cigarettes-on-their-butts monuments to an inconsistent collection of significances, and she was onto the red runway up to the sharp finger of the Light Pyramid in the distance. She could just run at that, hurl herself at it, and, like the two dowsers at the obelisk had said, the pyramid would project her negative energy up into the ether, and she would enter the Big Grid...

Two geese went clanking overhead.

Oh! K swerved violently to avoid colliding with a woman who had appeared on the red runway from the pathway on the right.

"Entschuldig..."

K stopped and turned back. Had this not all happened just before?

"Oh", said the woman in a pronounced German accent, "the young woman from bezide the Cornerstone Church! Is it you?"

"Yes, do we know each other?"

"No, I don't think so, I am not a... er... I am 'ere for a conference."

"At the Open University?"

"No, at the church."

"Oh. Religious?"

"Embroidery."

"Embroidery! OK. You're an embroiderer?"

"Obviously, I am."

"A whole conference on embroidery? What do you find to talk about?"

"O zere are many things. Are you interested in embroidery?"

K had never considered that question. But she suddenly felt as though maybe everything she had been doing for the past three days had been embroidery.

"Yes. Very."

"You know, ze remarkable thing about embroidery is that zere is no progress in it! No matter how complicated or sophisticated your cross stitches, knotted stitches, feather stitches, Zig Zag or Lazy Daisy, you will find precedent for zem from the beginning of time; embroidery came into the world fully formed and it has remained ze same ever since..."

"Like a revelation?"

"You might zay zo. You might very well zay zo."

"I think I understand," said K. "I have one last stitch to make and then the programme will be complete."

It was not a loop, it was a stitch!

"Programme?"

"Pattern."

"Ah, jah! Wunderbar! Congratulations!"

Turn around and walk back up Deer Walk and immediately turn right up Silbury Arcade, turning right along the far edge of the exhibition space (with John Lewis on your left). Once past John Lewis, turn left along the arcade, passing many palm trees, crossing Gold Oak Walk, passing more palm trees, and exit Centre:MK through the glass doors ahead of you. Once outside, turn right and then left along Midsummer Boulevard; go to the far right corner of the parking area, then down the steps to the space under the flyover (Marlborough Gate). Turn left across the bridge over Marlborough Street, following the Redway around a circular privet bed, then through the MK Rose, designed by Gordon Young, and down the long walk to the Light Pyramid, designed by Liliane Lijn, on top of the Belvedere hill.

Suggested end point of Walk 6: Light Pyramid, Belvedere, Campbell Park.

Walk 7

Suggested start point: Light Pyramid, Belvedere, Campbell Park

Estimated walking time: 3 hours

Walk around the Light Pyramid and turn back down the walkway in the direction of Centre:MK but, almost immediately, take the turn to your left along the path that soon bends around to the left and downhill. Follow this path through Campbell Park; where it splits into four, follow the main path straight ahead, taking the path passing to the right of the 'Onwards and Upwards' sculpture. You have a view to the cricket ground to your left. Cross the bridge over Overgate, then take the left-hand path, then straight on at the next crossroad of paths, then straight on at the Allen Jones metal head, and cross the bridge over the Grand Union Canal. Go straight down the steps on the other side and bear slightly left, across the grass, hugging the boundary of Gulliver's Land.

Making her way through the park, which briefly had the feel of a country estate – had they faked a Capability Brown-thing, or swallowed one up? – K was taken aback by the figure of a woman in the sculpture consumed by leaves. They looked unnervingly like feathers.

Beyond the park, K peered through the wire fence of Gulliver's Land. There was a spaghetti ride, an open wooden building like a rough stable with a non-traditional family (porcelain lion, lioness and two Buddhas, one gold and one grey), a copyright-busting mouse, an American jalopy, an elevated ride with pedal cars on tracks, an Asian family pedalling furiously went slowly round, but it was too like what everyone said about swans and K ducked through the car park entrance. The timber for the wooden barriers still bore the supplier's name and stamp; K had expected more attention to illusion. Perhaps it made sense if you paid for admission.

K followed a set of fresh tyre tracks in the grass from the car park; they had zig-zagged across the path, churning it up, carved through a clump of trees where a sign was knocked askew, and into the Cathedral of Trees. Like following stitches in the green. In the nave, mired, was the lowered chassis of the boy racer's modified saloon. Its dropped suspension had wrecked on the stone paving. The car steamed; the boy racer was slumped over the wheel, a beanie pulled down over his face. Unhurt, he was probably hiding his feelings, she thought. K ignored the accident; had he been trying to run her down and mistimed his attack? Or was he still lost and looking for his fellow hoons? She didn't care.

On a single slab of paving, joining the four thorn trees of the Cloister, were swirls of whitish lichen; like maps of galaxies and nebulae, more dust and grime than light. Back in the nave, K patched into the structure; it was the combination of organic and architectural that was getting to her. It seemed to her that the Cathedral of Trees had skipped ideas and was trying to fill the gap not with things but with living beings. K walked down the centre aisle, the limes, cypresses, maples and oaks unfolding, until she stumbled and sloshed out through the back of the altar and into a deep puddle and an inundated moat. On her progress down the nave, she had passed a woman leaning with her forehead against one of the maples; a man stood by, holding the space for her.

There was something that K was feeling toward here; something embroidered and organic, something that was patterned but also was just there. She knew that narratives like the car crash had nothing to with it; they were a 'smoke and mirrors' distraction. But they told her that she must be close to the answer, and that further intrusions and interruptions would be on the way.

In the drive way to the Nipponzan Myohoji Buddhist Temple, two large pieces of concrete, infill of potholes, had become dislodged and cracked. They looked like broken masks to K; messages to give up ideas that the programme was hers, that she was anything other than a part of the programme; the programme wrote her, not she the programme.

The fake stone circle nearer the lake was ridiculous; but that was its point. That it was in such absurdity and outrageous self-deception – or even knowing fakery – that the true patterns were to be found. But these ideas were far too 'clever' and far less convincing than the idea of a stitch. The three electricity cable covers (PO for Post Office), mounted on a double plinth – the same pattern as Lenin's Tomb, the toy soldier's tomb on the Wolverton Road and The Point, based on the immortal cube – were more authentic.

K climbed the steps to the pagoda. Joggers fussed at the foot of the steps. On the side of the white platform K waited patiently while a mother and her two children completed their game of catch with a large soft plastic pink ball-cum-balloon. A woman was blowing bubbles for a child to catch: "cheeky bubbles!" yelled the little girl, as the petrol-coloured spheres eluded her lunges. The white platform, set on a single two-dimensional plane, floated in the grass; it was the transcended form of the concrete platform K had stood on at the beginning of her journey, in the shadow of Bannatyne's gym. Climbing on to it, just a little higher than a normal step, K felt it take off and raise her up. She gazed out across the vista, over the flat surface of Willen Lake, under the curve of the blue sky, and the city appeared to her as a number of platforms, each one floating independently, but each moving in relation to all the others. There were green platforms, tree platforms, homelessness platforms, digital platforms, railway platforms, platform shoes, software platforms, hierarchical platforms, sporting platforms, gladiatorial platforms, intellectual platforms, research platforms, theatrical and poetical platforms, monumental platforms, retail platforms... the city was a dance of platforms. K stood and enjoyed it.

As with Siddhartha, enlightenment came not from luxury, self-denial or study, but by staying still, waiting, and seeing what happens.

Turn left through a gate with Disneyesque turrets. Cross to the far side of the car park and turn left along Livingstone Drive, almost immediately turning right (crossing Livingstone Drive) at the sign to 'Tree Cathedral'. Now bear left to the far left corner of the car park, take the path to the left and immediately take the left fork. This path bends around into the nave of the Tree Cathedral. (Be careful, when wet the flagstones here can be very slippery.)

Halfway down the nave, turn right into the Cloister area, walking the square marked out by the four Glastonbury Thorns, then return to the nave and turn right along the central aisle and out through the arch of fir bushes, across the grass and turn left along the path.

Take the underpass signed 'Willen Park'. Turn right along the path signed 'Newport Pagnell' and turn right through the underpass signed 'Willen'. Cross the Redway and turn right up the drive to the Buddhist Temple, passing the 'Hiroshima' sculpture by Ronald Rae on your left and the 'Medicine Wheel' stone circle on your right. Carry on past the Temple entrance on your left, along the Redway, passing a low concrete platform with three metal covers on your left. Turn left up the steps to the Peace Pagoda and climb them to the white tiled platform just before it.

The path began abruptly in the grass, passing the photo and flowers marking the sad demise of the Reverend Handa. His 'peace walks' over, but his heavy walking boots still worn beneath his robes, he was caught beneath the blades of his runaway tractor-mower. K was frightened by the thought of chaos and amputation; what if all her careful assembling of embroidery, platform and pattern were to run away with her?

> **Take the path to the right of the pagoda (as you stand with your back to the lake), passing the shrine to the Rev Seiji Handa on your right. Turn left at the T-junction of paths, then turn right at the next fork in the paths, walk up to the bench dedicated to Janice May Lambert, with a view down to Willen Lake Maze.**

The Maze was a current battlefield. Some combatants racing around the pathways, others cutting across its lines, a series of contests were in progress or regression. The rat was taking on the boy racer, his stuttering saloon rescued from the cathedral was slithering about on the grass while the suited giant rodent attempted to grab the wheel. Bill the Triceratops charged the unworldly Sandy Napier, who drove the saurian back with simple spells. There were a set of puzzling players that K remembered noticing in a mural on a pillar above Bannatyne's, despite all the fuss of no-budget filmmaking: a one-eyed something, a spaceman with a blank visor, a petrol pump full of flowers. All these things were now a part of the battle, taking the side of the Allies. Gabriel led a charge, commanding a huge force of lawnmowers that rumbled around the curve of the bowl rising up from the labyrinth in the base. The ghost of the priest was beside himself. The planner in the wheelchair was hurling pieces of Robert Hooke at the goggle-eyed shadow, to little effect. The legs of Samuel Kendal kicked the arse of the Rat in blind excitement; the Dog Poo Fairy was hurling handfuls of excrement at the Reverend Sandy Napier. The erratic rumbled down the side of the green bowl and crushed the Wall-E delivery drone. The blankness from the CCTV cameras came to the assistance of the planner, facing off with the shadow; blankness circled shadow, shadow stalked blankness, with little prospect of anything but a stalemate. One of the lawnmowers ran over one of Hooke's feet and pieces of blade swished through the air like shuriken; the priestly ghost and Hooke himself separated and were re-composed by the planner. The guide began to marshal the Superheroes, and with Gabriel's mowers in the vanguard one by one the Allies fell; first the boy racer who failed to check his wing mirror when climbing from his driver's seat and was sprayed in a crimson shower over the bonnet of his lowered speedster. The rat's tail was seared by sparks from a shower of philosopher's stone that dropped from the sky. If this was the 'war in heaven', K thought, it was attracting very little interest from the joggers and dog walkers who were skirting it on the paths above and below the Maze.

Except for one fellow.

K had seen the man as she climbed the path to the top. He was seated on a bench, on the very edge of the seat, writing in a tiny notebook, the kind you can buy in local post offices, with a cheap biro. He looked very pleased with himself as he scribbled rapidly, flicking over the pages as he completed one after another.

K went and sat beside the man. He wore a dark flat cap and mismatched waterproofs: trousers black, jacket dark blue. There was mud over his boots and around the bottoms of his waterproof trousers which had come undone, exposing the bottoms of jeans black with grime. K looked at his face and guessed he was at least in his late fifties, his blotchy skin and the bulge of stomach pushing the jacket outwards suggested he was a drinker, weak-willed, not much of an exerciser; his eyes were rather watery denoting a dampish character, a sentimentalist. It was part of K's work to judge accurately by appearances.

"Enjoying it?"

"I think it's going OK."

"Glad you're entertained."

"Well, it could be tighter, have more of an unfolding narrative..."

"Really? You sound quite the expert. Do you study heavenly conflict? A professor of theo-artillery, are you?"

"I'm a writer."

"Written anything famous?"

"No."

"That's a shame. Maybe your next one will ... you know... be your breakthrough piece... Working on anything at the moment?"

"Oh yes."

"What?"

"This."

He gestured to the battle below, which had begun to break up into individual conflicts with the priest baffling the guide who fell to her knees hyperventilating and the lawnmower squadron, commanded by an aerial Gabriel, bearing down on the hapless one-eyed something. The shadow and the blankness continued to cancel each other out.

"You're writing *this*?"

The writer lifted his pen from the paper. The battle below froze, a piece of the one-eyed something in mid-air flight. Gabriel hung over the green bowl, wings wide open, incandescent with beauty.

"Yes."

"Christ on a stick, who are you?"

"You won't have heard of me."

"What's your name?"

"Phil Smith. See, I said you wouldn't have."

"No, you're right... So, what is this that you're writing?"

K waved her hand over the freeze frame battle.

"It's the final few pages of a novel about a saleswoman called K, I'm nearly there..."

"Can I look?"

"If you want."

K walked around the back of the bench and began to read from the pad. The last thing he had written was in speech marks: "You're writing *this*?" He began to write again, the battle cranking up to full speed in the valley of the Maze below, as he continued to describe the novel to K: "...she's suffering from the delusion that the marketing campaign she is working on contains some kind of secret of life, and she's gone off on a kind of fugue, a psychotic journey, in which she is trying to find the secret key to the marketing programme in the landscape of this cit..."

K grabbed the bottom slat of the bench and with all her strength wrenched it upwards, levering it forwards, tipping the author onto the grass and sending him rolling down the slope, his portly body speeding his descent into the path of the lawnmower squadron which made short shrift of him, his pen, pad, ink, cap, blood, bone, split infinitives and awkward metaphors, all scattered in a pink blizzard of literary mash-up and cheeky bubbles.

The battle continued without its author, presumably, but K had turned swiftly away. Murder was murder, in anybody's book. She hurried to get down from the hill and into the town, away from all Superheroes and Allies and their Creators.

As K clumped down the steps she could feel herself shaking stuff from her character. "Delusion?" Of course she was effing delusional, who wouldn't be if they had some half-arsed, unknown fiction jockey ramming their head full of under-cooked ideas and motivations! But he was gone now and she could be what she wanted to be; there would be no more surprising and uncharacteristic notions popping into her head.

Now she would choose what she thought. She would let go of her guilt about her mother's insistence that she 'do something significant'; she would let go of her deep satisfaction with neatness, all that 'getting with the programme', and the sentimentality and idealism that she was supposed to have accrued while addictively watching Bollywood movies. All those were stereotypes that had been given to her by an author who only very approximately knew her, who only very approximately knew anything!

Well, he was dead and gone and she was already someone else; innocent in every way.

There would be no more mind versus matter, imagination versus desire; artificial conflicts to create dramatic tension. She had broken through to the other side of that narrative and she was free; and for reality she had the city and her journey.

"You might have created me," said K aloud to no one and nothing in particular, "but I am real now, these steps make me real, these trees, this bridge, these cars..."

> Turn back the way you came and immediately take the right fork in the path and then turn right down the hill, following either the zig-zag path or the steps down the hill. Go straight on at the bottom across the bridge over Brickhill Street, with a view to a pink, round building in the far corner of the field on your right.

K let herself into the field, just to rejoice in its grasses, flowers and ferns, to acknowledge their part in being her. But she had barely taken a step inside the gate when a fox stole out of the hedge. The two fugitives stopped, shared a look. Yeh, I could be any of that, thought K: foxy, vermin, outlaw. The fox trotted away, and with a glance back, disappeared into the hedge. Elusive. She wouldn't mind trying that on for size. She wondered if she would still fancy Amir in her new skin, and him her. Even though the author had been messing with her, she had felt really bad about leaving Amir in the churchyard at Little Loughton. Or would she get off with the Archangel Gabriel? Nah, that really was the author's fantasy and not hers; it was not necessary for her to be or do anything special – even 'elusive' was really the fox's to be, not hers – there was magic enough in her everyday.

As she walked on, not quite sure to where now, she began to soak up the terrain around her; she had thought at the scrambled start of her journey that her sudden super-sensitive seeing of ordinary stuff – brambles and coats and mounds of earth – was a kind of symptom, a side-effect, but she had been wrong. That was how characters in novels behaved; as if the world were background for them, something that made them stand out. For her now, the world was something that made her sink in. The soggy bridleway she crossed was a part of her, the leaves of the poplar honour guard along the canal edge turned lime by the Sun were part of her.

The same for the concrete kidney built for the BMXers, the tiny brick sun, the two-dimensional sheep that made her laugh when it became like the blade of a bacon slicer. Ponderous, meaningful or just funny, they were all possibilities for her and for the world she was part of. More sun shapes. Not so funny. Just being didn't have to be easy.

She could be difficult and conflicted too. Breaking free of your creator was not a solution, it was a platform, like the concrete one, like the magic one at the Pagoda, but what you chose from the landscape, that was you.

There was a faded notice in a poly-bag, tied to a lamp post. Calling out DOG FOULERS (an odd way of putting it), it was illustrated by a black silhouetted head with a white question mark in the middle. Nice touch. Very 'classy', K thought. She didn't have to approve of everything, but she had a power now to see everything. A tattered blue plastic bag caught in a tree, shaking with wounded fury. She saw, she loved. It was a poor thing, but it made her feel like a rich person, rich like a nice *arany galuska* cake.

K had not forgotten about the last stitch in the embroidery. That was not such a bad idea. She had made the connection with the needle-like Light Pyramid, and now she could see it again, the top of it against the clouds, way across the Portway, through the trees. She threaded her way through a double rank of silver birch beside the Redway; what might have scared her before need not scare her now. She did not want to hide behind a shadow. She wanted to bend back to a light that she felt fall upon her –

how long ago was that? – two days, three days ago? It was a long time to be changing; and she wanted to settle now. K was gathering so many things to her, but she did not want them to become burdens.

Pass Camphill Café on your left (a good place to stop for refreshments, open Monday to Friday, 10am till 4pm) and go over the bridge across the Grand Union Canal. Go straight on, through a play area and across Colesbourne Drive, then follow the path across Thorneycroft Lane, go straight on at the crossroads of paths, and then go over Oakley Gardens and over the bridge over Over Street. There is a view to a distant Light Pyramid on your left.

A murmuration of starlings flew in under the bridge and began to hunt around the verges and in the road. That was more like what she could become. A woman all in black was making her way along the gutter of Darley Gate and K thought, yes, it is possible to make a life like starlings. Grasses had rooted in a crack in the Redway. The parapet of the bridge over the Portway was a landscape in itself; K thought that she was simply crossing it to get to the Light Pyramid, but there would be no more 'simply crossing'. K could have written the story of her life without leaving the bridge, in grand tours of the thick forests of moss, voyages to the archipelagos of lichen, ascents of the mountain ranges of concrete. She even challenged a simulacrum-god that was presiding over the ritual circling of the roundabout below. A person did not need an identity; an ecology or a geography, two words for the same thing, were enough.

K skirted the Labyrinth in the park. People were wise, they made their own rituals; that's why these sacred spaces were barely used or badly used, if at all. Why did they expect people to trust artists and planners, when programmers and sales execs like her, or cleaners and security guards, made much better prophets. She might be in charge of herself now, but she was not sure that if she gave herself up to some artist's labyrinth those other characters – the alchemist, the rat, the erratic – would not try to loop back too, and tangle her in their mazes again. Up until now she had been nervous about looping back, because there was only the past to loop back to, but now she had 'previous' with the material of the city, she could feel that everything else had been a 'run up' to really leaping in. She had a foundation to push off from, a depth to dive into.

> At the next junction of paths bear right and cross Pastern Place, then cross the bridge over Darley Gate and go straight on, turning left across the second bridge over the Portway. Then take the right-hand path where there is a fork in the paths, walking under a footbridge and then under the flyover carrying Silbury Boulevard and take the left-hand path and then the right-hand fork up to the Labyrinth.

There were huge waves of metal on her horizon; the unfinished rebuilding of the art gallery, she loved the giant negative-Sun in its side, sucking in light rather than pumping it out, a box of gravitational collapse; for a moment she was tempted to dive in there instead. Each of the things – giant steel bug, multi-million pound rebuilding scheme, fox, grass in the crack in the tarmac, brick pattern in the side of Downs Barn – was a feather in her wings.

For a while K climbed down and sat in The Cave and wondered about what she should do about all her options. She would get back to her flat soon enough, get the taxi she should have taken in the first place, a neighbour would phone for a locksmith to let her in; once she had her spare set of keys she would collect the car, unlock her phone and accept that offer of having dinner cooked for her. Then she would run a bath.

Her first time through the Park, it seemed a minute ago and a lifetime away, she had intended to run along the ridge to the highest point in the city, the Belvedere, with the intention of throwing herself at the Light Pyramid, in the hope that she might be alchemically transformed from a negative energy into one of... what? Pure light? Angels' feathers? A decent person? And disappear into the cosmos? She suspected that her aim had had something to do with all the Napier stuff and seeing patterns every-where, but there was no author to end the story and cheat the physics now, no charlatan magician making it all up in a notebook. Of course, even when there was, it had not quite worked out as planned; she had been interrupted by the German embroiderer who had sent K off on another lap, to make her final stitch. Question was: did K have what it took to stick the needle in. If she threw herself at the Light Pyramid now, without any support from the themes or fantasy of the story, what would happen then?

She was in two minds; split, she went and stood on the brink of the final run to the Light Pyramid.

The two minds parted, at that brink.

After walking the Labyrinth, leave the space on the opposite side from where you entered and take the left-hand path at the fork. There is a view to the Light Pyramid on your left and to Xscape, the Theatre and the Art Gallery on your right. Go through the metal gate on your left and pick your way very, very carefully (it can be very slippery) down to The Cave (created by Ivan and Heather Morison); sit on the metal stool inside The Cave and consider the view. Then go back up to the path through the metal gate and turn left and then bear left where this path meets the Redway.

~#~

Suggested end point of Walk 7: walkway to the Light Pyramid, Belvedere, Campbell Park.

If you choose this route it will add 15 minutes to Walk 7.

~#~

If you choose the first mind of K, then take the right-hand turn at (and this side of) the black metal fence and posts (just before the final section of path to the Light Pyramid) and follow this path around the edge of the grass Amphitheatre auditorium, turning right and then left onto and along Avebury Boulevard, past the Campbell Heights flats on your left and, after approximately 100 metres turn right and cross Avebury Boulevard at the central reservation and carry on down the pathway immediately ahead of you until you reach the roundabout at the end of Highbury Lane, bearing left around the roundabout and taking the first (almost immediately blocked) road turning on the left. Continue straight on over the grass and soil mounds. This is accessible by foot. At the T-junction turn right along Smithsons Place (closed to traffic) and you are in 'the zone'...

Her first thought was for the place, the zone of the city, she had no mind to vaporise and lose its realness. It was the details of the city, the hole in the gallery, the fox, the lichen, the flapping of the plastic bag, the metal wave on the horizon, the beautiful Willen church and the amputated plaster arm, those were the things that gave her new being. Taking the first tangents, the edge of the auditorium, the little path off Avebury Boulevard – the same Boulevard she was on at the very beginning of her journey off the grid three days before, now at the other end of the centre – in minutes K found herself deep in the thicket and body of her own being, on roads reclaimed by grasses and shrubs. She was walking down a deserted, rampantly tree-lined boulevard, in a Pripyat-kind-of ghost town in the heart of an English city. But she was no ghost; she reached out to brush the heads of the grasses with her fingertips and nudged the uneven brick pavoirs with the toes of her shoes. At Woughton on the Green, K had fantasised about what might happen if MK were to become a fairy ring, but it already had, and here it was and she was deep in it...

If you choose this route it will add 2 minutes to Walk 7.

~#~

If you choose the second mind of K, follow the Redway to the Light Pyramid.

K's second thought was to go for it, to try for transcendence. Forget dinner. With the passing of the programme, and the company and Tracy Renshaw and the rest of the other plot exigencies of her author, nothing was keeping her in this world. But there might be another, a better.

Two geese, clanking, flew overhead.

K took off, decisively, running at full tilt at the white needle, sprinting so as not to lose her thread, the land either side easing and spreading; the circular pond, the grassy auditorium, the Chain Reaction sculpture all seemed to step back to let K complete her trajectory. Even the Sun was loosening and sinking. There was a cry from a sky so blue it was turning white. K was not even sure if it had come from her, and just before she hit Liliane Lijn's Pyramid, the Stone Swan settled heavily onto the red path between her and the needle of light.

"μὰ τὸν κύνα! I've caught the little δρομάς!"

But K could fight her own battles now, and with two deft moves she tore the Swan's wings off His carved shoulders and with the heel of her left foot she sent His mottled torso barrelling down the Belvedere ridge and into the circular pond at the bottom.

K lifted the two shorn wings above her head and, as though powered now by angel breath, she raced the last few metres at full tilt at the Pyramid.

Just before she smashed into the sculpture, Gabriel materialised alongside her, a Gabriel uncertain and unsure – partly the archangel keeping the chemists from their worst mistakes, and partly the handsome hobbyist with laughable interests – she leapt into his arms and they spiralled up into the blue and disappeared in a web of contrails.

Afterwards

K was never missed after that. Indeed she was never really known of. The illusion created by the errant particle of light had barely registered in MK; it was waved away. Like all its other photon-citizens, reflected each morning in the giant screens of Station Square, their reality depended upon their alchemical ability to sustain matter and hope, and K had both succeeded and failed in that particular superposition.

So, after finding her way back home from the ghost town between Avebury Boulevard and Childs Way, and into her flat, a sales exec took a bath, and let her boyfriend cook her dinner, and, later, in the golden hour of light, they drove to old Loughton where he took pictures of her by the church; but those were just two ordinary MK people who nobody gives more notice to than anyone else, absent from the novels and the movies, disappearing into the collective amnesia of the corporations and their offices, into the anonymity of the spectacles any city creates.

K's plan was sold all over the city in meetings, pitches and contract signings over the coming weeks. Among other commodities, many bathrooms were shifted as a result and what happened in their waters was often far from trivial or homogenous.

In the city of light, everyone is an exception. A cheeky bubble in a vacuum, borrowing their energy just to exist. The moral is: never pay it back. The field is yours...

The Sun shone again the day after K disappeared. The shoppers looked, bought and looked again. The spectacle had always been better than the real thing, everyone knew that; the central exhibition centre was always most exciting between exhibitions. The art in the gallery would never improve on the emptiness of the hole in its wall.

But those who knew how to ride the opportunities of light – simultaneously waves and particles – would never be bored, never be limited, for they knew that the city was simply a pin cushion, a building with a million doorways; life was a Swiss cheese. K had taught them, for despite (maybe because of) her disappearance, she was mistily and dreamily remembered by those who feared for the ground of their own being. She had become the city, and if you knew how to build your nerves around her grid, then MK could connect any pilgrim to a cosmic body, and then angels... even archangels might come!

That morning, the fourth since K took a sip of coffee and began her adventure, smokers at the INTU entrance on the boulevard milled aimlessly, unable to quite put their finger on the itch. But in the gap between the grey wooden fence and the giant planter, a tiny fringe of chipped orange paint began to glow and glow and glow and glow...

About the Author

Dr Phil Smith is a prolific writer, performer, urban mis-guide, dramaturg [for TNT Munich], artist-researcher and academic.

He has written or co-written more than a hundred professionally produced plays, and created and performed in

Photo: Rachel Sved

numerous site-specific theatre projects, often with Exeter-based Wrights & Sites, of which he is a core member. He has collaborated more recently with choreographers Melanie Kloetzel, Siriol Joyner and Jane Mason.

He is Associate Professor (Reader) in the School of Humanities and Performing Arts at Plymouth University.

Phil has published papers in *Studies in Theatre and Performance, Performance Research, Cultural Geographies*, and *New Theatre Quarterly,* co-authored a range of Mis-Guides with fellow members of Wrights & Sites, and written/co-written other books including: *On Walking …and Stalking Sebald; Walking's New Movement; Making Site-Specific Theatre and Performance; Mythogeography; Counter-Tourism: The Handbook; Walking, Writing and Performance; A Sardine Street Book of Tricks; A Footbook of Zombie Walking; Rethinking Mythogeography; The Architect-Walker; Walking Limping Stumbling Falling; Anywhere* and the novel *Alice's Dérives in Devonshire.* Fuller details of his work can be found at:

www.triarchypress.net/smithereens

About the Publisher

Triarchy Press is a small, independent publisher of interesting, original and wide/alternative/contextual/radical thinking about:

- organisations and government, financial and social systems – and how to make them work better

- human beings and the ways in which they participate in the world – moving, walking, performing, growing up, suffering and loving.

Triarchy Press has published a number of books about radical, performative or alternative walking (by authors like Roy Bayfield, Alyson Hallett, Ernesto Pujol, Claire Hind, Clare Qualmann and Phil Smith). For details of all of them, visit:

www.triarchypress.net/walking